THE LIFE AND TIMES OF "FLY-DI"

DIANE HOWARD

authorHOUSE®

AuthorHouse™
1663 Liberty Drive
Bloomington, IN 47403
www.authorhouse.com
Phone: 1-800-839-8640

First published by AuthorHouse 11/16/2009

ISBN: 978-1-4490-3491-7 (sc)

Printed in the United States of America
Bloomington, Indiana

This book is printed on acid-free paper.

DEDICATED TO

MY MOTHER,
THE LATE SYLVIA U. HOWARD
MAY SHE REST IN PEACE.

ACKNOWLEDGMENTS
THANKS TO THE FOLLOWING:

To my mother who-always reminded me that I could be whatever I wanted to be or do whatever I set out to do!

Gregory Dobbins who encouraged me to share my story and for always bweing there to hear my cry.

Travis Cunningham who listened to me when I first became pregnant with this idea and I shared with her. She encouraged me to give birth to the book so that I could tell my story and establish God's glory.

To my two older children Ta, and Monee and my nephew ka, I thank them for understanding the need to write this book and the encouragement they gave me and the green light to go with it.

To my sister and brother, who also understood and encouraged me to follow my dream.

To Jimmy W. Thank you so very much for all of your time and patience, writing and re-writing the manuscript and you didn't have to do it, but you did it and again I want to thank you so very, very much.

And to my niece, Nickcole who had to turn around and type it on a floppy disk.

Last but not least, to my daughter Teoka who assisted me with the title and my adopted God Son Timothy Bowden who drew my picture for the cover of this book.

FLY-DI 1
(FORMATIVE YEARS)

Life started out for DeShawn in a New York City Housing Project called Fort Greene located in the downtown area in the borough of Brooklyn. The Fort Greene Houses were one of the first city housing built on a massive scale in the city of New York during the early 1940s. Each building in the entire project was either 6 stories high or 11 stories high, DeShawn lived in one of the taller buildings.

The housing complex offered all the amenities of a small city, a hospital, public school, Jr. high school, High School, police station, fire station and a church, but growing up in the project wasn't very easy.

Housing maintenance workers who the tenants called porters .did an incredible job of keeping the huge buildings cleaned on a daily basis. Parents also made sure that their children complied with the housing rules because any violation of the rules meant being issued a $5 fine, which was then added to their monthly rent, an amount most parents considered extremely excessive. So most kids learnt early in the projects from their parents that if they were issued a fine it would be ass-whippin time"

Back then in the 1960s & 70s times were hard for most blacks that had migrated from various parts of the south to cities up north such as New York, but DeShawn's parents had migrated even further than most being from an Island country of East West Indies called Barbados.

Husbands could be seen leaving through out the project in those dark early morning hours going off to work everyday. A large percentage of these men worked in the ship yard not far from the project which was known as the Brooklyn Navy Yard, but DeShawn's father was different because he was one of the few black men in the city who actually worked for the New York City Transit Authority as a Bus Driver. Going off to work hard at whatever jobs they had was simply a sign of the times to bring home the bacon so that the wives could fry it up in the pan.

Through DeShawn's young eyes whenever she saw her mother in the kitchen preparing a meal, she was always reminded of the story in the bible when the Lord took 2 fish & 5 loaves of bread and fed all the people, well with a bag of flour her mother made miracles happen on a daily basis. Those meals may not have been a gourmets' delight with all the fancy fixings, but they were good, so good in fact that DeShawn could not ever remember missing one meal not one single day. Her mother taught her to always be thankful and to give thanks for whatever state they found .themselves in.

Being the last of five children and the baby of the family was not very easy because she felt asthough she was always under a microscope with everybody monitoring her every move! Playing outside with other kids or jumping rope her girlfriends would suddenly blurt out, "There's your sister" or "Your brother is watching you jump", but she wasn't being watched because she could not be trusted, she being watched for her own safety and health.

DeShawn had been a very sickly child since birth which included her being allergic to infant formula, whole milk, powdered milk and carnation can milk, the only milk that she could digest was soy milk and in those days soy milk was very expensive ,a can and that seemed to make her father very unhappy.

Her formative years were a constant reminder of her inability to tolerate milk in general and how expensive soy milk was in particular because of the dissension, conflict and strife it created for her mother whenever she had to inform her husband that they were approaching the last can of soy milk.

The scene was vividly etched in DeShawn's memory as her mother stood passively by each and every time listening to her husband go on and on about how expensive the milk was or how DeShawn had been sick with one thing or another since birth.

Yes DeShawn was on soy milk for about the first 10 years of her life however, her mother always managed to keep a smile on her face and a song in her heart. She would always pat DeShawn on her head and never forgot to give DeShawn words of encouragement and little affirmations like, "trouble don't last always" or "it will get better by and by" as she watched the pain and guilt that DeShawn displayed for being sick and making her daddy spend all of his money on her milk.

As DeShawn grew older her situation appeared to worsen she developed cronic asthma and was allergic to all types of things from dogs and cats to grass and weeds and on and on. DeShawn had been under the premise that as she grew older her health would improve and eventually it did. DeShawn was about 11 years old when she started becoming very aware of the situation around her. She began to make her own choices in the area of what she could eat and what she could not eat. She remembered finding out that she was allergic to chocolate, that happened to be her favorite candy. DeShawn would eat the chocolate and then break out into these fine prickly rashes. Her mother always knew when she ate something that she had no business eating and would nurse her back to health.

As time went on things began to change in DeShawn's life, her mother was always around along with her sisters and brother, but it appeared to DeShawn that her father's face had become scarce in the place. She began to think that her illness had caused her father's disappearing acts. How wrong was she, her illness had nothing to do with her father being (MIA) missing in action.

It started out with her father coming in late from work, then it became later and later. One night turned into 1 day and 1 day turned into 2 and it went on and on. Sometime she did not see her father for weeks on end. DeShawn questioned her mother about her father's disappearing acts and her mother would always say, "Oh, your daddy's working."

DeShawn remembered always having to meet her grand mother at the bus stop to help her carry the bags of food that she would bring all the way from 61st Street & Columbus Ave. in Manhattan to Brooklyn. She remembers wondering why Grandma-B was making so many frequent trips to Brooklyn and eveytime she came, she came with a care package. It took DeShawn a while to figure out if Grandma-B had to bring food all the way from Manhattan to Brooklyn it stood to reason that in DeShawn's father absences there was no food or money to purchase food, so grandma came to the rescue as a knight in shining armor, thank God for grand mothers.

Times began to get rough, DeShawn's mother had no marketable skills to offer to an employer due to- the mere fact that the only skills that she had mastered well was how to be a subservient wife and very loving and caring mother. If DeShawn's mother sounds like a saint, that she was! DeShawn's mother learned ways to help maintain her family and still be at home when her children came home from school.

DeShawn's mom became the baby-sitter for hire. She began watching this baby who lived in the same complex. The pay wasn't that great but it kept the food on the table and gave DeShawn's grand mother a break.

FLY-DI 2

Time passes by and as DeShawn gets older, she finally comes to the realization that daddy's gone and it had nothing to do with her continued illness or the cost of her milk. Growing older only led to the real deal of her dad's continued absence. Her mother continued to make excuses for her father's A.W.O.L. (Absent Without Leave) status. DeShawn became bitter and began acting out, her behavior was out to snacks and her 'I don't care attitude' left a lot to be desired, she was just totally out .of control and seemed to find comfort in fighting any and everybody.

Now school, let's talk about school. DeShawn did ok in elementary school but, when she got to Jr. high school her situation became worst! She was transferred from school to school she was in every Jr. high school in the district and out of the district as well. She could not control her anger, I think today that behavior is referred to as, 'Anger Management Problems,' but back in the days they did not label you as dysfunctional, or Mis 3, Speech Impediment, or, Learning Disable. DeShawn was just out of control and no one knew why.

As she grew older she became more defiant and non-responsive to all authority figures. There was even a time in DeShawn's life where she appeared to have had a death wish. She was unable to have healthy relationships and did not allow anyone to get close to her. DeShawn had 3 sisters and a brother, but she loved her brother with all her heart. He was the only one that could reason with her. DeShawn and her brother were always thick as thieves and there was no separating them. Everywhere her brother went she went, she always thought that her brother saw her as the brother he wished for, but never had.

DeShawn finally makes it to John Jay High School on 7th ave. in Brooklyn, joke, joke, joke. She lasted in that school for just about one year! Still angry and off the chain she continued to fight at the drop of a dime. DeShawn had one thing that she knew she loved and that was basketball, she loved to play basketball and was pretty good at it too. On the court she was able to run out her frustration.

DeShawn was a high school drop out with no direction and a great deal of built up anger with no way of releasing it. Her anger became worst, there were no anger management classes available to her, she was never taught an alternative to violence and how to redirect her anger.

The summer of 1964 was not a good year, DeShawn's behavior was just out of control, she continued to fight only this time she used whatever she had in her hand, one week she stabbed her brother's friend for putting his dirty shoes on her clean sheets on her bed, she had warned him!

The; next week she stabbed her then wanna-be boy friend for cutting her thigh with a piece of glass he found on the ground while they were sitting on the bench. When DeShawn stabbed Popalopa ;his mother did not press any charges however, Clayton's mother thought that DeShawn was out of her mind and was in immediate need of psychological help.

Clayton's mother pressed charges, the judge ordered an immediate psychological work-up. Low and behold the test results were negative, there was no evidence of any psychological problems.

The judge directed DeShawn to go home and return on the following day with her tooth brush. The judge went on to inform DeShawn that he felt that 18 months in a Youth facility would do her some good. DeShawn in her continued hostile manner informed the judge that he must be out of his mind if he thought if he sent her home for her tooth brush that she would return on the following day!

The look on the judges' face was one of instantaneous indignation and displeasure, but maintaining a sense of courtroom decorum he directed the court officer to take her away immediately. DeShawn's mother pleaded with the judge not to take her baby away, but it fell on deaf ears. The judges' stern facial expression of dismay as he looked at DeShawn indicated exactly what was on his mind, "just who the hell do you think you are speaking to in that tone of voice young lady!'

It became quite obvious that DeShawn had to be out of her mind and that she really was a troubled young lady to exhibit no regard for the judge, the person that held her life in his hands, the person that could make her life a living hell, the person who at this point was in total control of her future.

As she was being led out of the court room by the six foot two inch Caucasian man in his blue pants and starched white shirt she was unaware that he firmly held her by the arm. DeShawn moved trance-like and still defiant until she looked back over her shoulder at her mom and observed the look of pain, but it was the tears that ran down her mother's face that really hurt her the most!

DeShawn was escorted out into the hallway through a back door down this long corridor and came to another door that was locked which the court officer opened with a key from a big ring of keys. Entering she remembered sitting in that room for what seemed like an eternity until a woman finally came in escorted by the burly court officer who carried a tray with some milk and a bologna sandwich. DeShawn was indeed hungry however, she was allergic to milk and bologna always reminded her of raw franks. It was at that point DeShawn realized that this was not a dream and what appeared to be a nightmare was real and that there was no turning back.

The woman in the room was the psychoanalyst who was going to attempt to psychoanalyze DeShawn, what a joke. The woman never introduced herself or if she did DeShawn did not catch her name and that was because DeShawn was closed to everyone and eveything around her. The woman was a very passive, non-aggressive woman which was not a good thing for DeShawn. She remembered thinking that perhaps they should switch places because the questions that were being asked appeared to be questions that made no sense and had no substance to the here and now in her own reality. It appeared as if no one had informed the woman how difficult DeShawn was and in fact that DeShawn was not very approachable.

There was a man who had entered the room, but she did not get his name either. His questions were a little different but still did not make any sense as far as she was concerned. She remembered a response that she gave to one of the questions that he asked her. "If you see a train coming down the track and it jumped the track, what would you do?" DeShawn's response was, "Get the hell out the way!" DeShawn did not know if that was the response that he wanted to hear.,, but that was the response she gave. Another question asked that vividly stood out in her mind was,, "What does this picture look like to you?" while he showed her a picture that appeared to be a butterfly, but to her it looked like a bat and that was exactly DeShaws' response, "A bat, what does it look like to you?" is what she asked the man that was asking the questions.

It wasn't until much later when she found out that both the man and woman were again people who held her fate in their hands and they too would have the last say so. A short time later DeShawn realized that she did not do well on the question and answer part of what she later found out was her Psychiatric Evaluation.

FLY-DI 3

The Bus. The Green School Bus. DeShawn found herself on this green bus which reminded her of the yellow school buses that she used to refer to as the 'Cheese Bus' only this one was green. Little did she know that her destination would determine the next 18 months of her life. DeShawn recalled the feelings that she felt as they loaded the bus.

Yes, there were other girls heading to the same destination for different reasons. Everybody on that bus knew that there was no turning back! No one wanted to cry including DeShawn. When the bus pulled out of what appeared to be an underground garage and came up into the street and began to move out into the traffic slowly, DeShawn saw her mother walking down the block as if she was lost deep in her own thoughts, but the give away was in the fact that she walked with a heavy burden on her shoulders. She looked bewildered and lost as if she was walking in a daze back to her home. That now was the ultimate pain for DeShawn to see her mother in so much pain with that hurt look on her face and God only knows that ached she felt in her heart, now that hurt something terrible". It was at that point when DeShawn realized that her situation, was not going to get any better.

As the bus continued to travel down the familiar streets to get on the highway DeShawn wished that she could take it all back, but it was too late. DeShawn realized that for the next 18 months all of her decisions would be made by someone else.

The bus continued to travel and it seemed as though we were driving for hours and hours. However, in reality it had only been about 4 1/2 hours. By this time DeShawn was tired and she was famished, she wished that she would have eaten that bologna sandwich back at the court, oh well she thought it's too late!

FLY-DI 4
(FINAL DESTINATION)

They arrived at their destination. The house was huge, a great big house with a lot of land surrounding it, but on closer inspection DeShawn saw that it really looked like those houses she had seen on T.V., but a smaller version of that western program called 'Ponderosa' without the stables and horses. There was quite a few cottages on the grounds several feet a part from each other.

The bus driver said, "OK, everybody out one at a time, file out and stand in twos." DeShawn got off the bus first and waited for everyone else to step down off the bus. Once again DeShawn thought she was 'Charles in charge' and waited to be picked and pair up with a partner. The thought occurred to her about the person she was going to pair off with and whether or not she was going to become cool with the person. Every female on that bus had a problem, a very serious problem and that is why they were all on that bus going to the same location for the very, same thing; to be taught discipline and how to redirect their anger.

That residential program for girls was really called Valley Training School For Girls, but we all knew that those words were really dressed up and fancy words for a Reform School. The school was structured to teach girls with behavior problems how to behave. Yes, they had a school for academics, beauty culture and house keeping. The academics were taught by licensed teachers along with the beauty culture classes. However, on the other hand the house-keeping was done by the residents and they learned very fast because they had to clean their own room, kitchen and the hallways.

DeShawn learned very quickly how to buff floors by hand. She used to take turns buffing the floors on the very floor that she slept on. DeShawn had a great deal of difficulty adjusting to being a clean up woman because she had never did any house work at home. It was very hard for her to adjust not only to the house work, but to the discipline and instruction.

DeShawn had no regard for authoritative figures and was use to doing as she pleased, so adjustment was hard. She received a lot of tickets, misbehavior reports you got when you were not in compliance and after a certain amount of tickets came restrictions. When you were placed on restrictions you were not allowed to go in the recreation room, no T.V., no movies and the biggest restriction was when the house mothers went into town to do grocery shopping and you were not allow to go, that was the biggy of the biggys.

The only thing that they never restricted was your right to worship, the right to attend church. DeShawn went to church the first Sunday that she arrived at the reform, oops! I mean training school. She remembered not wanting to sit at the back of the church, wrong move! The preacher came out and stepped up to the pulpit and said with a heavy, raspy, ruff voice, "Praise The Lord Ladies" and she thought it very strange that no one said it back, there was no response from anyone. The preacher said it again, "Praise The Lord Ladies" and DeShawn remembered saying, "Praise The Lord To You Too", but she said it under her breath. There was something about the words Praise The Lord that stuck in DeShawn's head! She could not tell you what the topic of his message was that Sunday nor could she tell you what book he read from in the Bible. DeShawn could only remember that when he the pastor said, "Praise The Lord" it moved something inside of her.

DeShawn could not wait for Sundays to come. She remembered the pastor giving her a Bible, but she really did not have any knowledge of the Books of the Bible nor did she know who wrote each book and what the books represented. DeShawn just knew that there was a quickening in her spirit whenever she thought about church and the preacher and the words that he spoke. The pastor had a profound affect on DeShawn.

As time went on she began to change, her thought pattern was different, her demeanor was different, her willingness increased and her behavior was completely different from the behavior that she had exhibited when she first arrived at the school. DeShawn was not sure why the change was taking place, but she did realize that there was a change and that the change was for the good. The guard that she had up gradually came down. It became easier for her to make friends and to trust people again. During DeShawn's stay at the valley school it helped her to realize that she had been suffering from abandonment issues. She really missed her father, that was the root of her problem.

Through the grace of God, DeShawn continued her attendance at church and it helped her to deal with the issues that surrounded her and: her absent father; it was as if a brighter light that began to shine on her thinking, on her reasoning and on her spirit.

Disappearing acts, cronic illnesses, high cost of her milk were all thoughts she found herself thinking about for a long time. Little did she know that his disappearance had nothing to do With her cronic illnesses or the high cost of her milk.

As time went by and DeShawn began to grow into a nice young lady she began to like herself and realized that her father had left his family to become a rolling stone and she did not mean the singer. DeShawn realized that anywhere her dad laid his head became his home. She couldn't remember where she had read that 'A ROLLING STONE GATHERED NO MOSS', but she thought the phrase surely could be used to describe her father's disappearing acts in a surreal sense.

FLY-DI 5
(DADDY'S GONE)

It was not until DeShawns' life started changing for the better that she really began to realize that her father was really gone, he was not dead and buried in the ground, but gone and still she could not connect the dots.

The main reason she could not see the whole picture was simply because she was not aware of the other woman, the paramour, the significant other, the companion, whatever you want to call her; the home-wrecker. As DeShawn began thinking back she slowly started to remember the card parties that her father use to have, the women that use to be there, the drinking and smoking. DeShawns' father was something else. There was one woman that use to come to the card parties and when she came she would always ask DeShawns' brother and DeShawn to watch her money while she went to the bathroom. They watched her money alright! I think that she was aware of the fact that they always took a couple of dollars before she returned. Little did we know that she was the other woman.

As time went on it all came to light. The strangest part of the whole scenario was DeShawns' mother never drank, cursed, smoked or played cards! They say opposites attract. DeShawn found out much later that her mother was aware of the affairs and who her husband was with when he was not with her. If you let DeShawns' father tell it no matter what he did he always provided for his kids. Joke, Joke remember grand-ma and the rides from Manhattan to Brooklyn.

FLY-DI 6
(Learning True Love)

DeShawn's mother loved her husband, he could do no wrong! She took her wedding vows to heart. 'To Love, Honor and Obey Until Death Do You Part'. Those are the vows that she took and those were the vows that she took to her grave. DeShawn's mother's love for her mate was what DeShawn called truly unconditional. DeShawn remembered always saying to herself, "I never want to love a man the way my mother loved my father." She even went as far' as to say that her mother was a whimp, weakling, just too damn passive with her father because whatever he did was alright with her mother.

Her mother use to iron her father's pajamas. DeShawn would ask her mother, "Why, Why do you iron his pajamas, all he is going to do is wrinkle them up when he goes to sleep!" Her mother would just smile and say, "Oh girl, this is what wive's do" and continue ironing.

She remembered never being able to eat spaghetti or canned vegetables because everything had to be fresh this and fresh that! DeShawn fathers' excuse for not allowing spaghetti to be cooked in his house was, 'he ate so much of it while in the army'.. Whatever he wanted he got, he was the man even when he was M.I.A. and returned after a month or two, it was like nothing was wrong. Funny, DeShawns' mother really knew love and exhibited it at all times, but little did DeShawn know that she too would also learn to love just as her mother did.

Meanwhile back at the ranch, DeShawn learned to take short cuts back to the cottage. She learned how to buff the halls after waxing them. She would place one rag under each foot and begin to slide from side to side, in her mind she acted as though she was roller skating because she loved to do that.

While she was buffing the floors on her make believe roller skates she thought about the time her and her brother beat up this little girl who lived around the corner in the next building and attempted to take her skates. The girls' father came down stairs and grabbed DeShawn by her neck as her brother ran off and left her. Well the man took her around the corner to her father but he made the mistake of taking her around the corner with his hands still around her neck! DeShawns' father just happen to be home that particular day with a toothache. An event such as what was taking place in the projects spread like wild-fire through the grape-vine and made DeShawn's father aware of the situation before this man could reach DeShawns' building with her in tow. As DeShawns' father stood on his buildings' stoop waiting he observed the man dragging his struggling daughter towards the building with his hands still around her neck! A fathers' love. DeShawns' father jumped off the stoop like superman and beat this man like he had stole something. He beat the man bloody and never said a word to DeShawn or anyone. He just went back upstairs and went fast to sleep. A Daddys' love I guess; in his own way he loved his wife and his kids no matter how he lived his life.

DeShawn came back to reality and continued to buff the hallway. As time went on DeShawn began to love herself. During her stay at the Valley School she learned to. except the things she could not change. She also realized that life became so much easier if you just did as you were told. DeShawn also learned about sex. Yes sex, while she was away upstate away from boys and away from home.

DeShawn saw first hand bi-sexual relationships with the girls of the school, she also heard sex stories from the girls who were already sexually active. DeShawn while still a virgin never really thought about boys let alone sex. She wasn't really a tom-boy but she had never really thought about sex, boys, relationships, babies, lesbians that everyone called 'butches' or anything, all DeShawn wanted to do was reform, get it right and go home.

DeShawns' brother, where was he? what happened to the love that they had shared? DeShawn and her brother were very, very tight. They hung out together all the time. DeShawn remembered when she was first blessed with her menstrual at age 11, she told her brother and never told any of her older sisters or mother for that matter. Her brother had told her to go home and wait in the bathroom for him. He came back with this purple box of pads and he took one out and gave it to DeShawn and told her to put it on and exited the bathroom. When her mother found out that DeShawns' brother knew and did not tell anyone she was angry.

DeShawn really loved her brother, but she had abandonment issues with him too. She remembered when she first arrived at Valley School For Girls and getting letters from her mother and sister Daffy. She did not remember getting any letters from her brother, why? Did he give up on her or was he too busy doing his own thing? Reguardless, DeShawn loved her brother just like her mother loved her pops reguardless of what he did.

DeShawns' continued growth and self-exploration led her deeper and deeper into herself especially into those things that made her angry. She learned to channel her negative feelings. During DeShawns' stay at sleep-away school she did not have one fight. Yes, she got angry on several occasions and had wanted to fight, but she had learned well how to recognize her feelings by understanding why she got angry in the first place and what to do about whatever she was feeling at that particular time she was feeling it. Having learnt to express and identify the causes of her anger eventually led her to realize that most things that triggered her anger were not even worth her energy.

Her attendance at both church and school continued, but with a yearning to learn more about God and her very life. The change that was taking place inside DeShawn showed up on the outside as well.

She began noticing more and more as she went about her morning ritual of brushing her hair in front of the mirror that her reflection was radiating love back, yes she loved what she had became.

The staff at the school expressed their feelings about the positive changes that DeShawn had made and the positive person she had become. Her peers came to her for mediation, they valued her opinion highly. DeShawn afforded her peers clearer lens to see their own situations much clearer. Yes DeShawn loved who she had become and how well she had been doing in her program and even with her chores in her cottage. Yeah, things were beginning to look up for DeShawn and it was coming closer to her release date and she could not wait!

FLY-DI 7
(Departure Time)

DeShawn had gotten all the tools that she needed to become a productive member of society. She learned the tools to assist her with her anger, she learned that everyone that leaves her did not mean that she had did something wrong. She learned Consequential Thinking, she learned how to take time out and to think before she spoke. She learned that God, gave her 2 years and 1 month so that she could listen more and speak less. She left the school equipped to handle the trials and tribulations of life. The only thing they neglected to tell DeShawn was to take it easy, one step at a time, one second at a time, easy does it. They forgot to tell her that she can not play catch up. They completely forgot to tell her that the world had kept right on moving while she was gone and that it would not stop for her.

She was now 16 1/2 years old, still a virgin with no boy friend, oh wow! The day that DeShawn was released she went back to the only home she had ever known, her mothers' house. She welcomed DeShawn with a great big hug and a kiss and 2 eyes full of tears, but they were happy tears, tears of joy, glad to see her baby. Her mother while a little older still looked the same to DeShawn with her beautiful clear medium brown complexion and great big kool-aid smile which flooded DeShawn with pure emotions and feelings of love as she thought to herself, 'that's my mama'.

DeShawn was her mothers' baby, but by this time DeShawns' sisters were older too and each one of them had already had 2 or 3 babies of their own, oh wow! DeShawn started thinking where will she sleep? How is she going to live in this house with all of those people? DeShawns' dad was gone altogether. DeShawns' brother, where was he? another block! Her brother was her whole life. Growing up it was all about her and her brother, they were like frick and frack you did not see one without the other.

DeShawn is home, but she is unsure of what she wanted to do for the rest of her life, but one thing for sure she did not want to do and that was to be in her mother's house with all of her sisters and their children. On th£ very first day home the only one to greet her besides her mom was her sister Daffy. Daffy said, "guess what sis? guess who's home?" As Deshawn answered, "who?" she replied, "you remember Pa-Pa H?" "Of course," DeShawn said. DeShawn had had a school girl crush on him however, he was 5 years older than her. Pa-Pa H had been sent away to the big house for something he had not even done before she had been sent to Valley School For Girls and now he had been home a couple of months before she had come home.

DeShawn remembered being happy for Pa-Pa H because she knew that he had went away for something that he did not do. She remembered feeling very anxious about him being home and her hopes of getting a chance to see him and to see what he looked like. She remembered how tall, dark and handsome he was. Yeah, DeShawn really wanted to see him.

For some reason she began to remember the sex stories that the girls use to talk about in the Valley. School, their plans to have sex when they were released. She could never converse with them on that topic and she could remember being ridiculed for still being a virgin. The girls were willing and determined to give it up as soon as they were released, ironically even the girls that professed to be quote, unquote, "gay."

She remembered day dreaming all the time about seeing Pa-Pa H and what she would say to him. Well time went on day after day, week after week and she still hoped that she would run into him. DeShawn went up on the avenue where he used to hang out, everyone had seen him and talked to him except DeShawn. She even went so far as to put a A.P.B. (All Point Bulletin) on him.

So much time had gone by she wasn't even sure if he would remember her. She worried that he would think that she was still the little skinny girl with big feet. A sudden thought came to her mind as she thought about what he might think about her, she wondered what did she really want with him and why was it so important for her to make contact with him. Was he going to be her knight in shinning armor, was he going to be the man that took her virginity or was he going to be her way out of her mother's house or would he just be her friend.

DeShawn didn't have a clue as to what role Pa-Pa H would play in her life however, the need to see him was great and real in DeShawn's heart, mind and soul. The search continued and the hunt was on. DeShawn's determination grew more and more as each day, week and month went by. She simply refused to give up, whatever her motives were they were strong enough to keep her wondering, hoping, wishing and searching for him.

She knew where Pa-Pa H resided but she had changed, she was.not the same person that she was before she went away. She had returned home with an entirely different attitude. The old DeShawn would have went to his house, knocked on the door and when someone answered the door she would just ask for him. Today though' DeShawn has changed, she is determined to use Consequential Thinking.

She thought that if she knocked on the door and he answered it, what would she say? Suppose he said something to hurt her feelings, then what? She decided to play it cool and wait until they ran into one another. The hunt continued. It seemed like months had passed, but it was really only a couple of weeks.

DeShawn waited patiently for the day to come when she would be able to see his face close up, check to see if he still looked the same. The little cracked tooth in the front of his mouth would it still be there or was he still slightly bow-legged with his bell bottom pants? That thought alone made her reminisce back to a time when she would say to herself, "oo-oo-oo child", as she smiled at that private thought.

She knew that the day would come, she only hoped that it would be sooner than later. PatientS is a virtue that's what she had been told and learned and patient was what she intended to live with. DeShawn associated waiting to see Pa-Pa H with waiting for her release date from the valley school.

FLY-DI 8

The day has come and DeShawn finally runs into Pa-Pa H. The irony simply was that he had been right under her very nose all the time. As it turned out one of her sisters lived on the very same street that his brother did, only 2 blocks further up that street!

DeShawn did not have to wonder anymore what she was going to say because he was front and centered when they met. She remembers speaking first saying, "What's up? How are you? I heard that you had come home. So where are you living? Are you still living with your mother in the project?" He told her that he was still living with his mother, but that he trys very hard to stay away from the project. He also said that he spends a great deal of time catching up with his brother and trying to make up for lost time. Then he said real smoothly, "And how are you? you looking better than ever and I heard that you just came home from boarding school." Keeping her face serious on the outside while laughing to herself on the inside she answered, "Oh, that's what you call it!" DeShawn wasn't being coy but she remembered being very guarded and careful about questions that she asked.

Respect made Pa-Pa H something special in her eyes especially since he had taken the rap for his best friend and went to jail for. it. DeShawn thought of her past situation and determined her incarceration had been a life saver.

Moving right along, DeShawn swapped numbers with Pa-Pa H and as they departed he going one way she the other the urge for her to just turn around to get one look at him walking away with his slightly bow-legged self in his wide bell bottom pants was almost too much to control, but she did because she did not want him to know that she was watching; it took all the will power she had not to look back.

As she continued walking away she wondered to herself whether he looked back at her. When she rounded the corner she took the telephone number out of her pocket and at a single glance she was able to memorize it. Later DeShawn wondered who was going to call who first.

DeShawn was tempted to call him several times however, she decided to wait for him to call her first, she did not want to seem so anxious so the wait was on. The following night he called.

DeShawn's oldest sister answered the phone while she was in the bedroom thinking about the phone then she heard her sister call, "DeShawn, DeShawn the telephone." As she came out of the bedroom going for the phone her sister made the snide remark, "And don't be on the phone long because I'm expecting a phone call." In those days there was 'no-calls waiting'. DeShawn remembered saying to herself, "Now who in the hell do she think she is? What makes her phone call more important than mine?" That made her real angry.

She picked up the phone and said, "Hello?" with a real attitude until she picked up on the voice and became weak as a lamb covering it up with, "Oh hi, how are you doing?" He replied, "I'm OK, what are you doing?" DeShawn said, "Oh nothing I was just cooling out in my room." She dared, not mention that she was just in her room thinking of him. The conversation was real brief and they hung up.

DeShawn went back to her room and continued her thoughts about the man that she thought that she would marry and spend the rest of her life trying to make him happy just like her mother tried to do with her father, when for some unexplained reason the sudden thought of her being away at valley school and all of things it had taught her barged its way to the front of her mind, it had never helped her with the fear of dogs, four legged dogs not men.

Just as quickly as the thought came it left her mind and the last thing she remembered before drifting off to sleep that night was how her mother always tried to make her father happy by doing special things for him.

Keeping his house squeaky clean, taking care of his children, washing and ironing his pajamas only for him to wrinkle them up again when he went to bed, but none of those things ever seemed to be enough for her dad. The more dear mama gave the more her dad took, he was never satisfied. It was like trying toget blood out of a turnip. She never wanted to be like her mom, knowing that her mom loved her dad more than she loved herself, crazy or was it? In some ways DeShawn thought her father thought that he had done something special by allowing her mother to be a house wife and never having to experience the work force.

The following morning opening her eyes her mind immediatedly picked up the thoughts of last night - whoopty do, her mother worked like a government mule at home and never received any monetary gain nor did she get any acknowledgments like, 'well done my good and faithful servant.' Yeah, DeShawn wanted to love and be loved but she did not want to be nobody's slave. She remembered how sad her mother use to look but she always managed to hug and kiss her children and to remind them of how much she loved them and that there was nothing in the world that she would not do for them, even if it meant being someone's slave, 'her husbands'.

Moving right along - DeShawn continued to spend her idle time thinking about when and if she would get together with Pa-Pa H. She attempted to go back to school and for a while it was working out. She attended school everyday and her grades were fairly good. DeShawn attended school in the Park Slope area of south Brooklyn. At the time of enrollment the school was predominantly Caucasian.

Being enrolled in that school created some serious problems for DeShawn. She began to experience feelings of being in the wrong place at the wrong time, she felt a sense of not belonging, she also felt as though she always had to compete in order to stand out. DeShawn knew that she stood out being the only female in the school with corn rowed hair however, she wanted to stand out in the area of high grades.

DeShawn continued to attend school. She worked very hard to keep up with her grades and she was in her senior year of high school when her and Pa-Pa H finally took their relationship to another level. It was in the month of December when it finally happened!

DeShawn remembered that it was her sister's birthday and her sister asked her to baby sit her children so that she could go out to celebrate her birthday. "Why not", DeShawn remembered saying, "I might as well watch those brats because her and Pa-Pa H did not have any plans." It was about 7pm that night and as she was walking to her sister's house because her sister had told her to be there by 8pm, DeShawn had to walk two blocks after getting off the bus toget to her sister's house. But as she began walking down the block and turned the corner Pa-Pa H was coming around the corner, if she did not know any better she would have thought that her sister had set this entire accidental by chance up.

DeShawn said, "What's up?" "Where are you going" Pa-Pa H said. "I'm going to my sister's house", she informed him that it was her sister's birthday and that she was going to baby sit while her sister went out to celebrate. Pa-Pa H only smiled and said, "Ok, let me walk you to her house." "Alright," DeShawn said.

And so they began walking down the block when all of a sudden a dog, a big black dog, her worst nightmare came charging out of this gate they had just passed. DeShawn is petrified of dogs and cats. She took off running like she use to run track back in jr. high school and she was pretty fast. She made it to her sister's house with the barking dog right on her heels, but she out ran it and slammed the front gate closed as she flew up the steps to the house and locked the door behind her.

A few seconds later Pa-Pa H arrived at the house laughing, he thought it was so funny. She remembered him asking how did she learn to run so fast. DeShawn's sister came into the room and asked what happened? Pa-Pa H was laughing so hard she explained what had just happened because she did not think that it was funny at all.

DeShawn's sister invited him to join her for a drink in • celebration of her birthday. DeShawn had to baby sit so she could not drink and besides remember she was only 16.5 years old.

Pa-Pa H wished her a happy birthday, tapped his glass against DeShawn's sister's glass and wished her many, many more. DeShawn's sister thanked him and began to express how happy she was that he was home. She told him how good he looked and she even mentioned that he did not gain a pound and they both laughed and then she said, "Okay, Pa-Pa H good to see you but I have to go now." DeShawn's sister said to her, "Don't forget to lock the door when he leaves and don't open the door for anyone, I'll see you when I get back." She got to the door looked back and said, "The kids had their dinner already and they are ready for bed. Good night and have a nice evening", smiled and went out the door. DeShawn continues to wonder right up until the writing of this book did her sister plan the meeting between her and Pa-Pa H.

She locked the door and invited Pa-Pa H to have a seat, she turned on the T.V. and the rest was history.... DeShawn remembered punching Pa-Pa H in the face and really losing it. She remembered him saying to her after it was all over, "Oh, I did not know that you were a virgin!" She was so angry that she thought she was going to lose her cotton picking mind, one because it was nothing like the girls had talked about at school and two, it was very painful and she did not feel any of the fire crackers in her head the girls spoke about, no spell bounding sensations, she did not feel like she was going to the moon! instead it felt like pure hell. All she knew was that she had experienced the most excruciating pain and to top it off he did not even exhibit any pity or remorse when he realized the damage that he caused and not to mention the mess that we made, if you know what I mean.

All he could say to her was, "Oh man DeShawn, I did not know that you were not sexually active." DeShawn looked at him as though he had 2 heads and commenced to beating him down.

DeShawn assumed and you know what they say about assuming, Quote, "You make an ass out of you and me." Unquote, that with age comes wisdom, wrong because he was just as inexperienced as DeShawn was although he was 5 years older than her, do the math!

DeShawn remembered thinking that sex was just as over-rated then as it is today. All DeShawn remembered feeling was shared embarrassment, she was trying to understand how something that should have been so wonderful turned out to be so awful, not to mention very painful. She remembered saying to herself, "What the hell happened? Was that all? Where is the rest?" Something had went totally wrong here as she was left wondering was there more to come?

She remembered being so angry after the 60 second/1 minute ordeal and then the boxing match that she just asked Pa-Pa H to leave her sister's house which he did without saying a word. DeShawn was in such a state of shock shortly after he left that she sat down and attempted to figure out what the hell she was going to tell her sister about the fluid that resembled blood that was all over the sheets.

DeShawn did not have a clue as to where her sister kept her sheets, towels, wash cloths, etc. or how was she going to clean up this mess before her sister came home. Well lo and behold DeShawn heard the click of the lock and the turning of the door knob was when DeShawn remembered saying to herself, "it's all over now, it's my sister and .she's going to hit the ceiling and tear the roof off this house with her screaming." DeShawn realized right then that there'was no where to run, no where to hide so DeShawn just sat back and waited for the ball to drop.

DeShawn's sister entered the house and DeShawn asked, "How was your night?" Her sister replied, "Oh girl, I had a good time, I must have danced to every record that they played and all I want to do now is take a bath and get my tired butt in my bed."

DeShawn's heart fell to the floor at the mention of bed, she started hyperventilating and her hands began to sweat and shake, but after a moment all she could say to herself was, "Oh well, I might as well tell the truth because she is going to know anyway."

DeShawn sat waiting for all hell to break loose when suddenly her sister came out of the bathroom after taking her bath and went straight into her room without even saying good-night.

DeShawn sat on the couch and turned off the light waiting quietly in the dark for the explosion hoping and praying all the while that her sister would think that she was asleep and would not bother her that night, she even remembered saying softly to herself, "Wishful thinking." She fell to sleep that night sitting up waiting for her sister to come out the bedroom full blast, but it did not happen.

The next morning as the house came alive DeShawn said to her sister, "So you really had a good time and danced to every record?" "Yeah girl! 'Do you know the last time I went out dancing?" she asked. Before DeShawn could even answer she went on to say, "Let me tell you something and do not take what I say to you with a grain of salt. Girl, you better have fun while you can, you are young and you have your whole life in front of you. Take advantage of your youth because once you start having children your whole life stops completely, no more partying, no more hanging out with your friends and your life is no longer yours. So take advantage of your freedom and most of all get an education."

With that said DeShawn's sister cut her eye at DeShawn and made a stern frowned up facial expression and added, "Did you hear what I said?" "Yes I hear you" DeShawn replied and that was the end of the conversation. DeShawn had waited for the punch line, but it never came. DeShawn's sister never brought up the situation that took place the night before. It was evident that she knew what had taken place the night before because it wasn't hard to tell with the mess that was made, but she never said a word, even up until the day she died. That was their little secret and DeShawn appreciated not having to explain the mess that was made.

DeShawn had listened carefully to every word that her sister had spoken. She understood that having children was no joke and particularly if you were not married. Little did DeShawn know that her sister's speech came too little too late.

DeShawn wondered why her sister never said anything about that night, was it because she really loved and approved of Pa-Pa H? or was it because she could relate to what happened as a girl thing? who knows! Well day by day DeShawn thought about what her sister told her. Each and everyday DeShawn thought about what took place that night, as a matter of fact it was pretty much all DeShawn thought of, for one it hurted so bad, two was the unconcern Pa-Pa H displayed, not to mention the fact that he totally neglected to use a rain coat if you know what I mean! All of that rolled around in DeShawn's head. Each and everytime that she spoke to Pa-Pa H she could not believe that she felt so angry with the man that was the love of her life.

The following month DeShawn waited for her period to come. She waited and waited and finally she realized that she had messed up big time. No period in any language equals you're pregnant, you're having a baby! DeShawn could not believe what was happening to her, a baby, that's crazy she thought, I'm still in school, I'm not old enough to have a baby, let alone try to take care of a baby. I'm a student with no job or husband and as soon as my mother finds out that I'm pregnant I will be homeless too. DeShawn went to panic city!

She decided not to tell anyone her secret. She remembered the speech that her sister had given her however, it was too late. DeShawn decided to call Pa-Pa H bn the telephone to tell him of their dilemma. She did not want; to talk to him over the telephone because she was afraid that someone would over hear their conversation. DeShawn told Pa-Pa H that he needed to come over as soon as he could because she needed to speak to him about something that was very important. His reply was positive, he said he would be over as soon as he got off from work.

DeShawn's anticipation led her to think what was he going to say? She remembered talking to herself outloud saying, "I don't care what he say I'm not killing my baby." DeShawn's waiting that day felt as if time was crawling along ever so slowly, but finally 5 o'clock came around and her thought immediately flew to the fact that Pa-Pa H was off work.

However, it took him an hour to get home and he was not stopping at his house but coming straight to her mother's house where DeShawn lived with her mother and all her sisters with their kids along with her one and only favorite brother, who knew nothing of DeShawn's situation. DeShawn waited for her knight in shinning armor to come, eight hours had seemed like an eternity but he finally arrived.

FLY-DI 9
(THE WELL KEPT SECRET)

Pa-Pa H knocked on the door. DeShawn answered, "Who?" knowing good and well who it was. She was waiting for him to arrive at her house however, after he arrived she remembered wishing she had never asked him to come over because suddenly she froze up and did not really want to talk about anything.

She tried to think of something else that she could talk about that would hold some serious intent and she could not think of a thing. All of a sudden DeShawn became very angry at herself for punking up and she just blurted it out, "I'm having a baby, I missed my monthly!" "You what?" he said.

"My period. I have not gotten a visitor in about 3 months," DeShawn replied.

Pa-Pa H looked at her seriously and said, "Stop joking." DeShawn rolled her eyes and said, "I wish I was joking, I'm dead ass serious and this is' not a joking matter!" He had this side ways' smile on his face and asked DeShawn, "So what are you going to do?"

DeShawn said, "What do you mean what am I going to do?" and with a very harsher tone to her voice and a dead serious look on her face she added, "I'm keeping my baby, what do you think?"

Pa-Pa H looked up with a complete full moon size smile on his face and said, "Are you serious? You're really gonna keep it? Are you sure that's what you want to do? Where is it going to sleep? What will your mother say? Did you tell your brother, what did he say?"

So many questions forced DeShawn to silence him with a look towards the walls. He immediately understood why she was alittle reluctant to"discuss their issue in greater detail in the apartment because walls have ears. They decided to walk outside so that they could continue discussing their current situation.

Once outside Pa-Pa H went on to say, "I would never ask you to kill our baby, I am just thinking about you and the ramifications that can come to you behind you being pregnant."

DeShawn said, "Let me worry about me, I can take care of myself."

DeShawn questioned Pa-Pa H about what his intentions were and what did he plan to do about her being pregnant. He stated to her that he intends to step up to the plate and handle his business.

DeShawn asked, "What business are you talking about?"

He replied, "Our baby!"

DeShawn said under her breath, "Yeah, that's what I'm talking about!"

Pa-Pa H continued, "I don't want no problems out of your brother, you know how cool you and your brother is, he's going to have a fit."

DeShawn said softly, "Yeah, I know that's why I haven't told him yet!"

DeShawn reiterated that she had not told anyone and that she didn't plan to tell anyone, especially her brother! She planned to let everyone in her family find out when they found out. DeShawn kept her little secret for a little while. Pa-Pa H didn't even tell his family. DeShawn and Pa-Pa H kept their secret, they both decided that they would keep it as long as .they could. They felt that if they could keep their secret there would be less drama, little did they know that they planned and God replans.

It was one summer afternoon when DeShawn made the mistake of asking her mother to straighten her hair. You see in those days there was no perming or weaving of hair. You straighten your hair with a hot comb and Royal Crown Hair Grease. Think back, you know! You place the hot comb on the stove jet and waited for the comb to get red-hot and then you pulled the hot comb through your hair. If you had hair of fine texture you could straighten your hair with a little Royal Crown and a good brushing.

Well DeShawn's mother began to straighten her hair on this summer afternoon while DeShawn sat on the floor between her mother's legs who was sitting in a chair when suddenly DeShawn attempted to jump up from between her mothers' legs. Her startled mother said, "Girl, stay still. Where are you going?"

DeShawn could not say a word, before she knew it she had reguritated all over the place. With a look of concern and worry both on her face she asked her daughter, "Girl, what's wrong with you?"

DeShawn replied, "I don't know mommy, it must be something that I ate."

She looked at her youngest daughter and said in a sweet, kind and loving voice, "You must be pregnant and I'm going to tell your father."

DeShawn remembered thinking to herself, 'tell my father! you don't even know where my father is, how are you going to tell him anything and besides he left us, he don't know whether we're coming or going'. But because DeShawn loved her mother so much she dared not talk back to her and she never wanted to say anything to her mother that may have caused her mother any pain. You see, DeShawn's mother was so sweet, so loving, so caring, so attentative to all of her children that to DeShawn her mother was the best mother in the whole wide world.

The thought of telling her mother that she was expecting a baby was very painful for her, but lying to her mother was worst. The well kept secret was out.' DeShawns' mother knew her daughter was pregnant it was a mother's instinct. DeShawn thought that her mother had known all along and that she was just waiting for DeShawn to tell her.

Well DeShawn fessed up and copped out to her mother's accusation about being pregnant. She watched her mother's face drop to the floor and mouth opened wide in surprise just for a split second as she recovered her composure to say, "Baby you're pregnant. Where are we going to put another baby in this house?"

DeShawn said, "I don't know mommy, but I am keeping my baby". By then DeShawn was 4 months pregnant.

DeShawn's mother said, "Wait till your father find out that his baby is having a baby, he is going to have a fit!"

She said to her mother, "Mommy, Daddy's gone, why do you keep acting like Daddy really cares about what's going on with us?"

She replied, "That's my husband and that's your father and you better not ever forget that! No matter what your father has done, he provides for us and he will keep providing for us".

DeShawn's mother evidently had forgotten that DeShawn was actually the one who talked her into going down to family court toget child support for her and her brother after her father decided to desert the family. DeShawn remembered forcing her mom to go and sit in the court room and waiting for the judge. Her mother had been nervous and very afraid, but she managed to stay.

When the judge finally came out of his chambers however, he did not have on a black robe like DeShawn remembered the judge that changed her life. The judge was very angry at her father for coming to court attempting to tell him what he was not going to do. DeShawn remembered the judge telling her father that he had his nerve coming to court refusing to financially support his wife and kids. The judge said to DeShawn's father, "Where do you work sir?"

"I work for New York City Transit Authority as a Bus Driver," he replied.

He then turned to DeShawn's mother and said, "What kind of work do you do madam?"

DeShawn's mother stated, "I am a house wife sir, my husband never allowed me to work outside the house".

The judge asked, "Is that true sir?"

"Yes".

The judge studied her father a moment and said, "That's why you are going to support your wife and those children. You will furnish your wife with your medical cards which will enable her to get medical assistance for herself and the children".

DeShawn could not recollect the dollar amount that the judge ordered her father to pay to her mother every two weeks however, whatever the amount DeShawn's father was totally pissed off. When court was over DeShawn's mother took a deep breath and actually felt good about what had just taken place. She felt so relieved because now she did not have to worry about how she was going to pay her rent or feed her children and her grand-children, remember all her sisters had 2 or 3 kids of their own and no one was married or employed.

After leaving the courtroom DeShawn and her mother were waiting for the elevator when her father walked up and said to DeShawn, "I know that nobody but you talked your mother into bringing me to court. She would have never thought of this on her own." DeShawn became very annoyed by the statement that her father made because he made it sound as if DeShawn's mother did not have a mind of her own or perhaps she could not think for herself. DeShawn simply said, "Oh well, handle it."

DeShawn and her mother proceeded into the elevator, her father caught the next one. In the elevator DeShawn's mother cautioned her about disrespecting her father and what the Bible said about honoring thy mother and thy father. DeShawn replied, "I know mom, but the Bible also states that parents should not provoke their kids."

Her mother smiled and said, "You have been reading your Bible."

DeShawn loved her mother with all of her heart. She knew that eventually she would be leaving her mother's house sooner than later and she really wanted to know that her mom would be alright because there was no more meeting nanny at the bus stop and there was no more care packages because nanny had passed on to glory. Somehow DeShawn knew that she would be alright as long as she knew that her mom was alright.

As time went by DeShawn's mother became more confident in herself. Her mother's self-esteem had risen far beyond DeShawn's wildest dreams.

DeShawn's mother started baby sitting for the little girl next door, all was well, her mother even smiled alot more than usual.

It's summer time, the sun was out, DeShawn was big, pregnant and showing. Her father came over to visit the family. He realized that DeShawn was really having a baby, he'd seen it with his own 2 eyes. DeShawn remembered her father looking at her with disgust in his eyes. She did not know whether the look was due to her pregnancy or was it because this was the first time that he had seen her since they left the courtroom and the judge demanding him to do his husbandly duties.

She recalled looking at him as though he had no business being there. Finally he said, "So what do you plan to do?"

"Do about what?" was all she could reply because she didn't have a clue as to what her father was referring to when he asked, so what are you going to do?

Her father replied, "Are you going to keep that baby and be just like your sisters with all their babies and no husbands, . living off the system?"

DeShawn said that she had no idea what system he was referring to and that she definitely planned to have her baby! Well, her father's reply knocked her for a loop when he said in a voice . of great disappointment to his favorite baby daughter, "You're either gonna get an abortion or you're going to leave my house!"

When she heard that she thought to herself, 'How is he giving me a direct order when he no longer lived in the household and has been gone for a good while?' Looking at her father through eyes filled with pain and disillusion she replied, "How long are you giving me to get out your house? because I am not killing nothing now or ever." His reply to her question was, "2 weeks." DeShawn looked at her father with disgust, disbelief and said, "Check this out, give me 2 days and I'll be out of your house!"

After calming down DeShawn realized that because of her anger and frustration in her father's demands she might have spoken in haste, but she had just felt so betrayed and let down in her father's final decision.

DeShawn remembered thinking about her 3 older sisters with their 2 and 3 children each and how her father never gave them that ultimatum, it just wasn't right. DeShawn was not sure how to handle her immediate situation, but one thing was for sure she was determined to keep her baby come hell or high water.

Later that night sitting on the end of her bed with her mind going a mile a minute she thought about being a high school drop out, but refused to even think about public assistance. She had no savings in the bank, the only income that may have been available to her was Pa-Pa H's which wasn't much. DeShawn knew in her heart of hearts that everything would be alright, but just how she did not know. She refused to give up and give in to the termination of her pregnancy which was suggested by her father.

Her mother was aware of the ultimatum that her husband had given to DeShawn and even though she was a very quiet and humble woman who had never once defied her husband in all her years of being married, she did not intend to let her baby have a baby and be homeless. The sad fact was simply that her husband no longer even lived there anymore.

FLY-DI 10

At this point DeShawn was 9 months pregnant and still living with her mother and daddy was still no where to be found, but from.time to time over the telephone he continued his verbal threats about DeShawn having to move out. DeShawn did not take her daddy's threats lightly because she knew that eventually she would have to move.

She felt safe even though her dad was not residing with them, but she knew that oneday he would make good on his promise and when she thought about it she knew that he was still angry at her for making her mother take him to Family Court for Alimony/ Child Support. With all of this on her mind she continued to make plans for her and her new baby. She had in her mind that she would stay at her mother's house until she gave birth to her baby and then she would find a job and move out of her mother's house.

It all sounded real good to DeShawn in her mind, but in reality there was already about 10 people living in the house including her and her brother along with her sisters and their children. She knew in reality that she had to get up out of that house as soon as possible (ASAP).

DeShawn continued to await the birth of her miracle child. In those days you were not able to find out the sex of your child while attending your regular clinic appointments. Everyone had to wait until they gave birth to obtain the sex of the child. Unlike today you can know the sex of the child way before the child is born, no more surprises at birth, it's a boy, or it's a girl, no more secrets.

DeShawn really wanted a boy however, she had resigned herself to the fact that whatever the sex of the baby was would be alright with her just as long as the baby was healthy it would be perfectly fine with her. Pa-Pa H really wanted a boy and that was all to it for real!

DeShawn waited patiently to give birth to her baby and even though she was still living with her mother and 9 months pregnant she remembered saying to herself over and over, "that she did not want to bring another baby into her mother's house.' She felt as though this pregnancy and her baby would be another added burden to her mother. She also realized that there was enough boarders in that house and there was really no more room for another head.

The night before DeShawn had made up her mind that reguardless of the situation at hand she would-not raise her baby in her mother's house nor would she be on public assistance and she definitely would not be a burden on her mother. Her mother was just the sweetest, kindest, gentlest person you ever wanted to meet and DeShawn refused to do that to her, bring another baby up in her house.

Bright and early the next morning found DeShawn in the kitchen preparing herself something to eat. While scrambling her eggs and onions in the frying pan.she heard the ringing of the telephone in the living room immediately followed by her oldest sister's voice calling out, "It's for you DeShawn and hurry up because I want to make something to eat also and I want to use the pan."

DeShawn heard what her sister had said but paid it no mind as she snatched the frying pan off the stove and placed it on the kitchen counter-top and hurried into the living room to answer the telephone. DeShawn would recall the incident vividly years later. She had not been on the phone 30 seconds when her sister suddenly flew into the living room frying pan in hand in a fit of rage talking complete trash. What she was saying made no sense whatsoever to DeShawn who continued talking on the phone.

At this time evidently feeling she was being ignored she attempted to actually hit DeShawn in the stomach with the frying pan, eggs and all! DeShawn at this point realized that her sister was not playing with a full deck and she had to protect her stomach and unborn child. They began to go for blows with her only thought protect her unborn child.

DeShawn had always thought that her sister had some anger management issues or some type of psychological issue, but this was not the time to attempt to try to reason with her, she was off the hook. During the fight DeShawn had dropped the phone, but she could hear Pa-Pa H's tinny metallic voice coming through it as it lay on the floor, "DeShawn, DeShawn are you alright?"

Just how long the fight lasted DeShawn did not know, but she remembered hearing someone pounding on the door as if they were trying to break it down, it turned out to be Pa-Pa H coming to his baby's mama rescue. He entered the house and asked what was going on? DeShawn explained to him that while she was on the phone speaking to him her sister became annoyed and began spasing out and attempted to hit her in her stomach because she left her food in the frying pan.

Pa-Pa H couldn't believe what he was hearing and he began to spas out too. He started ranting and raging about DeShawn's sister being crazy and how he did not want DeShawn living there and how he was going to get her out of that house.

The next afternoon DeShawn began to go into labor. She believed it was due to the stress and strain from the day before and the drama she went through with her sister. She called Pa-Pa H to inform him of the situation and he came immediately however, when he reached DeShawns' mothers' building and saw the ambulance he just froze up. DeShawn remembered the ambulance attendant telling her that they could not wait any longer and that they had to get her to the hospital. She wasn't trying to hear that, she wanted Pa-Pa H and she wanted him not now, but "right now", she said.

DeShawn was unaware of the fact that Pa-Pa H was right outside of the ambulance with her sister, but for whatever reason he did not want to ride in the ambulance. When she arrived at the hospital Pa-Pa H was right there.

The labor began, the pains stopped and started, they were intense, long and hard. DeShawn remembered praying for the pain to stop, but to give birth to a healthy baby. She really wanted a boy deep down in her heart, but at that point a healthy baby was her only concern. As the labor pains continued she remembered worrying about her brother and what he was going to say?

Just for a brief moment in between contractions DeShawn in her clarity thought, 'where was. her pal? her buddy? her friend?' She was really hoping that her brother would show up at the hospital, but he didn't. Knowing how very close she was with her brother caused her concern, afterall people had always said that they were still like frick and frack. The thought that they did everything together brought back the look on her brother's face in her mind when she had finally told him she was pregnant, it was her last conscious thought as a sudden bout of pain shot through her body and the labor began again.

The life and pain inside forced her to quickly dismiss that thought and concentrate on the life she was about to bring into this world. The more pain that DeShawn experienced the happier she became. She realized when she gave birth to this baby that her life would never, ever be the same again. The baby would change her life forever. There would no longer be just DeShawn and her way of life doing things her own way, love was about to change things, true love.

Giving birth to this baby made DeShawn contemplate thoughts that were profound, it meant forever letting your heart walk around outside your body. Now that was deep and from what depth this wisdom surfaced was a mystery, she could only instinctively reason that motherhood was a good thing in her mind. She was so excited about giving birth and having a baby that as the pain progressed DeShawn was determinded to push that baby out.

As the pain became severe the doctor kept saying, "Breathe mother, push mother, breathe mother, push mother!" Wow, the sound of that direction push mother really sounded good to DeShawn.

FLY-DI 11
(Here Comes The Blessing)

Up until this time things were so hectic around her with activity and dealing with the sudden flashes of pain that she was having trouble with what was reality or what was just a figmentation of her own imagination. Realization actually dawned on DeShawn during one of her intervals from contractions that she was going to really be a mother in a few seconds and her life would change forever.

There would be a female or male child who was always going to need her undivided attention. -She remembered saying to herself that if she gave birth to a girl, the girl better have a head full of hair and that if she had a boy she hoped that the boy would have her eyes and smile.

Lost in thought laying back' on the operating table, in the delivery room with her legs propped up in stirrups when suddenly all hell broke loose, the kind of hell that changes your whole train of thought. DeShawn remembered the doctor saying to his assistant, "Her water, broke." What water? What the hell are they talking about? But the most-vivid thought she remembered thinking was she felt as if she was urinating on herself.

Suddenly she saw the doctors putting on their off white colored latex gloves and pulling this blue colored mask down off the top of their heads to cover their nose and mouth. The doctor began to give a reversed order of command to DeShawn, "Breathe mother, but don't push, breathe mother, breathe mother, in and out, in and out, deep breathes mother, deep breathes, don't push mother, just continue to take deep breathes, we will tell you when to push. When we tell you to push mother just push as hard as you can." DeShawn waited for the signal and began to push. She pushed with all her might.

She remembered pushing 3 hard times on the count of, "1,2,3, push, 1,2,3, push, 1,2,3, push" and then it happened, a beautiful blessing from God. A 6 lb. 11 oz. healthy baby with 10 fingers, 10 toes and teasing brown complexion with eyes just like DeShawns'.

DeShawns' first words afterwards to the doctors were, "Let me see my baby, let me see, what is it? is it a boy? let me see." The doctors' only reply was, "Just a moment mother, let us clean him up." DeShawn being so excited exclaimed loudly, "It's a boy, for real it's a boy." Turning his head ever so slightly he replied, "Yes mother, it's a boy." DeShawn then said, "Can I hold him? Can I hold him please?"

Pa-Pa H did not know his son had been born because he was in the waiting room which was the custom in those days, fathers were not allowed into the delivery room.

The doctors began to clean up her beautiful blessing from God. As she watched them drop some eye-drops into her son's eyes and he began to cry out the attachment to her son began again right then and there. Leaning up on her elbows craning her neck in the direction of the doctors she vehemently asked, "What are you-all doing to my son?" The doctor replied, "Relax mother we are cleaning the baby up, we have to place these drops in his eyes to keep his eyes from becoming infected." She thought about that a moment and asked, "Infected from what?" The doctor simply said without taking his eyes off of what he was doing, "From the after birth."

Already DeShawn was being a protective new mother, she had already developed her motherly instinct to protect her child. She questioned whether the drops was making the baby cry. It seem as if everyone doctors, nurses and the various assistants were becoming a little irritable with all the questions that were being asked, the evidence was their facial expressions to one another, but on the other hand they were probably use to an over load of questions from a new mother.

In those moments it really sunk into her that there is no HOW TO DO MANUAL that comes with motherhood. She fell right in and became very overly protective of her new blessing from God, her son. DeShawn paid attention to every move her son made. During the cleaning of her son in the delivery room she refused to take her eyes off of her son. When the doctor took the baby over to the cleaning table she remembered warning the doctors not to get her baby mixed up with anyone else's baby.

She remembered the doctor directing the nurse to give her a sedative to calm her down and make sure it had a tranquilizing effect. DeShawn recalled fighting off the sedative until she observed the doctor placing the name label on her and her baby, that was the last thing she remembered before the exertion, excitement and sedative put her out for the count.

When DeShawn awoke it felt like she had been sleeping for a long time, but in reality it had only been about 6 hours. The nurse arrived to her room without her baby and the first question that came out of DeShawn's mouth was, "Where's my baby?" The nurse directed her to relax-and stated, "Mother you had quite a bit of stitches and you must relax." DeShawn was unaware of the fact that she had been given 22 stitches in the vaginal area which allowed her blessed baby boy to enter into this world, that fact amazed her.

The pain, stitches and fear, it had all disappeared in a matter of seconds once she was able to hold her baby boy, feed him, change him and even observed him with a smile on his face. Everyone use to say that DeShawn was imagining things, they use to say that a new born could not smile but she knew better, she had observed it for herself.

Feeding her baby was easy, in those days breast feeding was not pushed in the local hospitals in Brooklyn. She did not attempt to breast feed, she bottle fed her baby and he ate very well, as a matter of fact he was quite greedy or should I say he had a very good appetite. He ate every four hours on the clock. If you let him he probably would have ate every three hours.

DeShawn grew so attached to her baby boy, she never wanted to let him out of her sight, he was her pride and joy. She remembered watching the look on Pa-Pa H's face when he looked at his first born, his son, his man-child. Pa-Pa H had a very nice smile however, the only time you observed his smile was when you watched him watch his son. Pa-Pa H was a man of very few words but his actions spoke louder than words. He loved his son, you could see it in his eyes. Pa-Pa H came to the hospital everyday after work for the three days, but it was the forth day that we both were waiting for that finally came.

FLY-DI 12
(THE BUNDLE OF JOY GOES HOME)

Baby boy had everything he needed to enter into his new environment. It was late October and close to Halloween and she remembered when she was expecting her baby and she was given her due date of always hoping that her baby would not be born on October 31st, you know Halloween, witches, warlocks and pumpkins, but thanks be to God he was delivered before that dreadful day.

Motherhood was grand, the staying up late at night when the baby develops colic and is unable to sleep, constipation, gas pains, teething and the whole nine. DeShawn's baby basically was a good baby if he was not sick. She had a bassinet for her son however, the baby always slept with her. She kept her baby very close to her.

DeShawn's mother also watched over her grandson, she acted as though he was her all and all. Pa-Pa H's mother also loved her grandson, she gave him a nick name, she use to call Buzzy. DeShawn and her son spent many week-ends at his paternal grandma's house which was DeShawn's get away, her home away from home.

There she and Pa-Pa H and the baby shared very quiet special family moments together. There was no arguing, no over crowding and there was privacy. DeShawn-and her son continued to live in her mother's house with all of her sisters and their children along with her brother. All of her sisters had more than 2 kids apiece. In her own mind she knew it would not be long before she seriously had toget out of that crowded apartment that she shared with her mother, siblings and their children.

Everybody was sleeping on top of one another, there was no room for a crib. DeShawn and her baby began to sleep together in the same room with her sisters and their kids once he out grew his bassinet.. She realized that sooner or later but more like sooner she thought she would have to move.

Pa-Pa H really did not like the idea of his son being over DeShawns' mothers' house with all those people, but Pa-Pa H continued to take care of his business. Her baby had everything he needed because every pay day Pa-Pa H would come over DeShawns' mothers' house with pampers, baby powder, baby food with deserts and cereals.

Although her sisters were all older than she and had children of their own DeShawn was the only one that had a man who stepped into his fatherhood shoes and handled his business, but unknown to him DeShawn had noticed for some time that every time he brought those items to the house they would disappear and no one seem to know where the stuff disappeared to.

Days turned into weeks, weeks turned into months and it was around the time her son began to take his first steps that she knew it was time to go because eventually things had progressively worsened. DeShawn really, really loved her brother and her brother had his own room and oneday her son had just started walking on his own and being young and curious he used toget into everything, he knew no boundaries and he walked all over the place. On this particular day her son walked to the back of the house and just for that split second he was out of her sight when all of a sudden she heard him cry out in pain, DeShawn ran to the back of the apartment and her son was standing in the middle of the floor in her brother's room, he had a big red mark on the side of his face and DeShawn's brother was still trying to find a vein in his right arm.

DeShawn remembered becoming very very angry, she picked up her son, looked at the side of his face with tears running down her own face, she looked at her brother dead in his eyes and told him if he ever touched her son again she would kill him. As much as she loved her brother she loved her son that much more.

She realized at that very moment that she could kill for her son and that's it and that's all, motherhood had finally-reached its' full potential with her. That incident was the straw that broke the camel's back. She came out of the room with her son and yelled out to her mother, "Go in the room, look what your son did to my son's face, your son is a dopheine, look at him, he's shooting dope in your house, go see, why don't you go see?" DeShawns' mother was in denial, she did not want to believe that about her only baby boy.

DeShawn was so angry she really couldn't recall whether her mother looked or not, all she knew was that she could not stay there. She had to get out of there. First the stealing of her son's food, pampers and everything else that was his and second now this slapping her son's face, that's it, enough was enough, too much was just too much. She really did not want to tell Pa-Pa H what had taken place, with her son and her brother, DeShawn began to cry. She told him that it is time for her and her son to get out of that house. Pa-Pa H agreed.

The following week and during their visit DeShawn remembered reading the Sunday newspaper while her son was sleeping. She recalled looking at the back of the paper for apartments for rent. She was well aware of her financial situation however, she had great faith in her baby's" father and she knew that he would do whatever he could to make the situation better.

The need to get out of that house was pressing. DeShawn found herself every week-end at her son's grandmothers' house buying and reading the daily news. She knew that eventually she would get out of the situation that she was in. This one particular Sunday DeShawn was reading the daily news but she was looking for the sales and not an apartment. DeShawn knew that she was unemployed and not receiving any state aid. Pa-Pa H was working at the time for minimum wages and after taxes he would bring home about $125.00 aweek after buying tokens, pampers and baby food there wasn't too much left.

As faith would have it DeShawn was at the end of the paper when she discovered a page in the paper that read room for rent, Kitchenetts for rent, working people preferred. DeShawn began to get excited her heart started pounding, her eyes lit up like a Christmas tree. The kitchnette that was listed was 3 blocks from Pa-Pa H's mothers' house and it was also very close to DeShawns' mothers' house and the best part about it was the rent was only $82.00 a month, can't beat that can you?

DeShawn tore the ad out of the paper, she showed the ad to Pa-Pa H and he was just as happy as DeShawn was. DeShawn did not know how they were going to pay the rent but one thing she knew for certain was that she had to get out of that mad house. DeShawn remembered thinking how hurt her mother would be when she found out that they were moving. She rehearsed over and over in her mind what she would say to her mother.

She really loved her mother and didn't ever want to hurt her. Pa-Pa H and DeShawn called the number that was listed in the ad and low and behold an older man answered the phone. She could tell that he was an older man and that he was from the south by the drawl in his voice and the prononciation of some of his words.

He went on to question her about her employment, whether there were any children and was she married? DeShawn only answered 2 out of 3 questions, no she was not employed and she only had one child. DeShawn then quickly asked him how much was the rent? Although the ad in the paper said $82.00 a month she was eager to make sure that it was not a typo. She went on to explain that her baby's father was a full time employee with a very reputable firm and that they would really love to take a look at the kitchenette.

DeShawn was really confident that if she was allowed to meet with the landlord that she would in fact get him to see it her way and she did. The landlord gave DeShawn and Pa-Pa H the kitchenette, he stated that there was something about them that he admired.

He stated that because we were young and just starting out that he would work with us. We had to give him a month's rent and a month's security, once again Pa-Pa H made it happen.

Moving out was not that difficult, we had no furniture, no pots, no pans, no dishes, no nothing, all we had was a vision and a dream and with that we made it happen.

FLY-DI 13
(HOME AT LAST, HIM, ME AND BABY MAKES THREE)

We moved into our little kitchenette and DeShawn's primary-focus was family. Once again DeShawn had to grow up just a little bit more. She started keeping house, she turned a kitchenette into a one bedroom apartment. She put up a curtain between the foyer and the kitchenette area. There was no living room, just one big room. By the time DeShawn finished her son had his own little room, his private space.

DeShawn realized that she was totally dependent on Pa-Pa H and that was alright for the needs of her son however, it was not alright for DeShawn and her needs. She did not like the idea of depending on Pa-Pa H for all of her needs. From time to time her mother would give her a couple of dollars for her pocket.

As time went on the rent was paid, groceries were met and everything appeared to be going well and eleven months later here comes another one, DeShawn was pregnant again. She knew that another baby would make their living situation alot harder and there was still just one salary coming in. DeShawn for what it was worth never, ever entertained the thought of abortion.

DeShawn gave birth to her daughter and all was well, so well that DeShawn remembered thinking at times that she had the All American Family, one boy and one girl with the boy being the eldest, the only thing missing was the house with the white picket fence and the dog. Little did she know that all hell was about to break loose.

DeShawn never allowed her mother to babysit her children, not because she thought that her mother was not capable of caring for her children, but simply because her sisters had worn her mother out. It was as if DeShawn had twins the children were only eleven months apart.

She took her children everywhere she went. Pa-Pa H had a step father that really admired her independence and for Christmas he purchased a twin stroller for her and the children, what a blessing that was.

Time went on and things appeared to be peachy creme. Pa-Pa H went to work and she stayed home and took care of home. Never in her wildest dreams did she think that Pa-Pa H would ever do anything to hurt her or the children.

He had a habit of always hanging out with his friend Gotti and Big Ro and DeShawn never really gave it any thought because she didn't really have any friends. One day while she was visiting her mother her nephew who lived with her mother was at home and he said to her, "Aunty, I seen uncle last night he was at grandma's house with Gotti and a girl." DeShawn questioned her

33

nephew as to who the girl was? She knew that Gotti was dating her nephew's paternal aunt and she knew that Pa-Pa H was not stupid enough to bring his girl-friend to a place where everyone knew her. She was curious, but she just let it slide.

On another occasion DeShawn's nephew once again shared the same information. Pa-Pa H began coming in later and later in the evening and his excuse was that he was working, but his weekly checks remained the same. She found herself becoming weary and upset most of the time. So one day she reluctantly questioned him about this female that he was hanging out with over at Gotti's girl-friends' house which was DeShawn's nephews' grandmother's house. Of course he denied it, DeShawn wanted to believe him so bad and she did.

DeShawn had watched her father's infidelity with her mother and she hated it with a passion and she just knew that her man would not do that to her. Well let me tell you, she was wrong. One evening DeShawn was home with her two beautiful children while he hung out that particular evening. It was getting late and he was not home yet, DeShawn began to worry.

She had just gotten off the phone with her mother and the phone rang again instantly, DeShawn picked up the phone and said, "What did you forget to tell me ma?"

And the voice on the other end said, "Hello, is this DeShawn?" DeShawn replied, "Who wants to know?"

The voice on the other side said, "My name Drena and I am just calling you to inform you that I am pregnant by Pa-Pa H and I am quite aware that you have two children by him."

DeShawn replied back to the voice on the other end, "If you were aware of us how did you allow yourself to get involved and to get pregnant at that?"

Her reply was this, "Well my mother is going to make us get married and after I have the baby I will get an annulment and then you can marry him."

DeShawn remembered the pain that she felt in her heart. It was as if someone had stuck her straight through her heart with a thin sharp needle.

DeShawn"s reply to the voice on the other end of the phone was, "Oh that's what you think."

The voice said, "No, that's what I know, my mother will pay for the annulment after I have the baby because my mother has money."

DeShawn told the woman if she ever called their home again that her mother would be using some of that money that she has to bury her daughter and she hung up the phone.   .

DeShawn remembered crying her eyes out, hoping that the children would go to sleep before their father came home. DeShawn for some reason knew that Pa-Pa H knew that this woman was going to tell DeShawn. DeShawn figured at one time or another he and Drena had this conversation and he probably attempted to derail the telephone call. Drena felt that because her mother had money and they lived in a co-op that they were in control of everything and everyone.

DeShawn remembered pacing the floor, laying down and getting back up. She was waiting for him to come through that door, she waited and waited with much anticipation. She tried to figure out what his replies would be to the questions that needed to be asked, she could not understand it, she began asking herself why?

She just did not understand why she had not seen it, or had she seen it but chose to look the other way? She did not want to believe that her life was going to end up like her mother's.

She never anticipated being the mother and father in her family. Pa-Pa H was well aware of the pain that she felt watching her father cheat on her mother day after day, week after week, month after month, he knew she talked about it often enough. The more she thought of her father's infidelity and the pain she was feeling she began to get crazy thoughts in her head.

She thought about boiling some grits, yes, you know hominy grits and mixing some honey with it so that when she threw it on him it would stick and he-would burn slowly. DeShawn knew that that would not work because she knew that she did not want to go to jail and leave her children. Murder was out of the question but she wanted him to hurt just as she was hurting.

DeShawn felt a combination of pain, starting with betrayal, deceit and ending in dishonesty. DeShawn said to herself, he was my first and only love, "the sun rose and set on him, why would he do that? DeShawn waited and waited that night seemed like an eternity.

FLY-DI 14
(ALL HELL BROKE LOOSE)

DeShawn heard the key in the door, Pa-Pa H appeared to be having a difficult time finding the key hole, DeShawn remembered jumping up and opening the door and.as soon as she swung the door open Pa-Pa H entered the foyer which was their son's room. Before DeShawn knew it she drew back her fist and punched Pa-Pa H dead in his face. While she commenced to punching him she kept saying, "Why, why did you do this to us?" She kept proclaiming that she did not deserve that.

Pa-Pa H replied, "Please lets' talk, wait, listen, let me explain!"

DeShawn said, "Explain what? she's pregnant by you and her mother is going to make you'll get married until she has the baby."

Pa-Pa H replied, "That's what she told you?"

DeShawn said, "Oh, you knew that she called me?"

"Yes," said Pa-Pa H.

DeShawn questioned how she was able to obtain their phone number?

And he said, "Gotti gave it to her."

DeShawn stated, "Where are you coming from?"

Pa-Pa H replied, "Gotti's house."

She thought that's where my nephew always saw his uncle at with the other woman. DeShawn questioned Pa-Pa H about the information that she had obtained from Drena, the other woman. Pa-Pa H stated that he was not going to marry her and that he did not care what her mother wanted. He stated that he was not even certain as to whether or not the baby was in fact his. Pa-Pa H said that she was just like a door knob, everybody had a turn. That made it worse, he was having sex with a nasty girl!

DeShawn screamed and cried as though some one had just informed her that her mother had just met her demise. Pa-Pa H cried too! He began saying things to DeShawn, "I love you, I I want to be with you, get a calendar and pick a date and we will get married on which ever date you pick!"

DeShawn remembered saying, "Oh now you want to marry me all of a sudden because you got busted, now you want to get married?" But at the same time she was frantic searching for a calendar and wiping her snotty nose.

DeShawn managed to find a calendar and remembered sitting on the side of the bed while looking at the calendar while tears continued to flow from her eyes. Pa-Pa H sat down beside her and said, "Baby, I am sorry. Please, pick a date."

She hesitantly picked a. date, whatever that date was something was going on that day and Pa-Pa H said, "No, it can't be that day."

DeShawn began to spas out again and Pa-Pa H exclaimed, "Come on DeShawn, cut it out! I do want to marry you, I love you, that's just not a good date."

DeShawn said, "Ok, what about this date?" and Pa-Pa H was in agreement with the second date that was choosen.

That night appeared to be a very long night. DeShawn remembered not being able to sleep, she: was not sure whether the reason why she was not able to sleep was because she was still angry at the infidelity or for the fact that her and Pa-Pa H had picked a date for them to be united" as one. DeShawn was just falling asleep as day break came but. that night had been the longest night in her life!

DeShawn was tired as all outdoors. That day was one day that she wished that her son' had slept late. I know you're wondering what date did DeShawn pick? Well, the date was April 20th.

Day after day she began to plan for her wedding. Pa-Pa H did not have alot of money and neither did she. DeShawn's father had money and could have helped with the wedding expensives however, although he wanted DeShawn to get married, which was the honorable thing to do, he did not contribute because the man that DeShawn was marrying was from St. Thomas and not Barbados. Now on the flip side Pa-Pa H's father had a truck load of money and was tight as a church door on a Monday and he didn't really care for DeShawn or Pa-Pa H. She really did not care who liked her or didn't like her she was determine to make this marriage happen. She began to skimp on her pennies, she saved every extra dollar she could and finally she hustled up enough money to purchase her wedding dress.

DeShawn was always mature in her thinking far beyond her age. She really didn't have any friends but some how she was content with the fact that she matured early and had become a mother. DeShawn remember thinking back to how the girls that she used to hang out with all terminated their unwanted pregnancies. She reflected back to the ultimatum that her father had given her when he first learned of her pregnancy. It was like it was yesterday, "Get rid of it or move out of my house!" The scene was still fresh in her mind as she remembered asking her father, "How long was he going to give her to get out?"

So the wedding plans continued. DeShawn not having any friends but attempting to be cool with Pa-Pa H's sister she asked her to be her bridesmaid. DeShawn had a couple of sisters however, because the wedding was a very tiny one she could not ask one sister without asking all of her sisters, so she settled £ for Pa-Pa H's sister and I mean settled.

DeShawn remembered going to this store called Goodwins in downtown Brooklyn. Now DeShawn was the one that was getting married not Pa-Pa H's sister. There was no such store as David's Bridal at that time, she allowed Pa-Pa H's sister to pick out of the two dresses the color she favored and DeShawn took the one that was left, a pink dress. No she did not wear white, remember DeShawn had already given birth to a beautiful little boy and white was suppose to represent purity. Although she could not wear white because of what it represented she always knew that she had a pure heart and that was more important to her than any white dress.

So they purchased the dresses. Until this very day DeShawn still wonders why she allowed Pa-Pa H's sister to get first dibbs on the dresses. They were cool, but they were not that cool, but that's DeShawn with her giving heart always trying to please others before pleasing herself.

DeShawn went home and tried on her dress, she remembered calling her mother and sister Daffy and telling them about her wedding dress. No, the dress was not a long white dress with a trail, but it was her wedding dress. It wasn't what the dress looked like to DeShawn but it is what the dress represented.

Time went on and all of the preparations for the wedding had been made. The invitations went out to a selected few. DeShawns' mother was elated because DeShawn was the youngest of 4 girls and the only one to get married. Her mother was planning to prepare her famous peas & rice, along with her roast pork and ham for the reception, everyone was excited and so was DeShawn.

The wedding was scheduled to be held in DeShawns' mothers' living room. No, the wedding was not being held in a great big cathedral however, it did not matter to DeShawn all that mattered was she was marrying the father of her children her knight in shining armour, the love of her life, the first man that ever got so up close and personal .with her. The man that she wanted to spend the rest of her life with, Pa-Pa H.

FLY-DI 15
(HERE COMES THE BRIDE)

It was almost as if the windows of heaven had opened up just for DeShawn and her special day. The sun was brightly shining, the weather was unusually warm for an April day. The birds were beginning to hum what DeShawn thought was her wedding melody. In a couple of hours DeShawn was going to become the wife of the man she thought was her knight in shining armour, the only man that she loved and admired beside her father, the • man that she looked forward to spending the rest of her life with,

DeShawn was happier than a pig in slop and as the hours passed she was becoming more excited by the minute. She tried to play it cool, calm and collective however, it did not work. Although DeShawn had a very inexpensive wedding, very small, quaint and very few invited quest her excitement could not be contained.

Most of the quest were DeShawn's mother next door neighbors. Pa-Pa H's mother was never really excited about her son's choice for a wife! Little did she know DeShawn was not all that happy about gaining her as a mother in law and the in-laws that came along with the package. Although DeShawn and her mother in-law got along there was always something in the back of DeShawn's ; mind that made her keep her guard up.

It was DeShawn's wedding day and she was determine not to let nothing or no one interfere with her special day. She remembered thinking to herself and saying silently, 'her mother is here, her brother is going to give her away and that's all that counts." For a brief second DeShawn remembered all the hell that her father had put her through when he found out that the love of her life was from St. Thomas and not a Barbadian, like coming from Barbados made you a better person.

In retrospect and remembering DeShawn's father and the treatment of her mother by her father DeShawn could appreciate her financee', husband to be coming from St. Thomas. DeShawn continued to have pent up feelings about her father and the horrible treatment of her mother. She had a point she had to prove to her father and that point was she would never take no crap off no man, no matter who he was or what he had. She adopted a motto very early in her life which was she would never need a man to validate who she is or who she would become.

DeShawn had a determination that was beyond compare, she used to always say that she never wanted to be like her mother, never realizing till much later in her life that she was just like her mother when it came to loving her children and loving her man. Her mother taught her how to love completely but not unconditionally.

Getting back to the wedding day. DeShawn wanted her father to be there, present at the wedding not to give her away, but to show him that she. kept her baby and rectified the broken rule of having a baby before marriage. DeShawn did it her way.

The wedding was about to take place and seeing everyone assembled in her mother's tiny little project living room sent an electrifying thrill through her body. Her mother's apartment may have been small but there was a whole lot of love and warmth flowing around that little room. DeShawn remembered seeing her father's sisters entering bearing gifts, Pa-Pa H's cousin was there too, she really adored him.

Yeah, it was about to be on, everyone that was somebody to somebody was there. Pa-Pa H's best man and friend was present. She remembered how fly her brother looked in his olive green and brown plaid jacket with solid olive green pants and brown shoes, but for some reason she couldn't remember what color shirt her brother was wearing, but knowing him the shirt was probably solid brown. He was dressed to kill, looking like a model from G.Q. magazine.

DeShawn loved her brother dearly and he loved her tool Her brother was very overly protective over her and during their adolescence her brother kept a very close and tight rein on his baby sister. Right before the wedding DeShawn remembered thinking to herself hum, now I am grown and no one will be able to tell me what to do any more, not even her over protective gatekeeper hound dog brother. DeShawn realized that her brother meant well and she loved him for that.

Her thoughts were suddenly brought back to the immediate present when someone said, "Here comes the preacher!" Glancing at the clock on the wall told DeShawn the preacher was a little bit late. A quietness fell upon the house when the preacher entered the door and apologized for his tardiness, but no one really cared that he was late, all they cared about was the fact that he was alive and present to perform his duties.

It was always protocol for the bride to be a little late, but no way was DeShawn going to be late for her wedding. She was a little nervous and attempted to hide her fears, but everyone who knew her knew that she was not a punk and that it was just the brides nervous jitters that was taking over.

DeShawn looked around to make sure that everyone was in their rightful places. She heard the door open and she glanced over at it hoping that her father may have found his way to the wedding, but nope, wrong answer, it was another late guest entering the apartment.

Just then her brother walked up behind her and whispered in her ear, "Sis you do not have to marry nobody! If you marry him we will not be able to hang out anymore." He told her not to marry that chump, he let her know that her and her children would not want for anything and he gave his word that he would take care of us as long as she did not marry him. She looked back at her brother and said, "I love him bro., and it's time for me to make a family for me and my children." She was sure that she saw tears well up in her brother's eyes as he frowned up his face real tight attempting to keep the tears from rolling down his face.

DeShawn assured her brother that her and her kids would be alright and that the time was now at hand. The preacher began to gather all the guest while he began to teach the values of marriage. Trying to stay focused on so many things going on around her it was a wonder that she remembered the preacher saying that marriage is honorable in the sight of God and that it should not be entered into lightly. The preacher also stated that we should honor, obey, love and cherish until death do us apart.

DeShawn took her vows very seriously and the next thing she knew the preacher said to Pa-Pa H, "You may now kiss your bride." She smiledd as she looked her husband in his eyes and said, "I love you." DeShawn's mother was very happy however, her brother exhibited the same feelings that he had prior to the wedding, damn, why did she do that? why did she have to marry him?

The reception was cute, DeShawn did not have many friends so she mingled with her family, neighbors and Pa-Pa H's sister and her family but she could not wait for the reception to be over, she wanted to go back home with her husband and son. This was the beginning of her new life.

After taking pictures and opening up their gifts they finally went home. Oh, by the way there was no honey moon, but she was ok with that. Now, get this you recall the reason why she and Pa-Pa H so hastily picked a date for their wedding! DeShawn could not forget it. She remembered reminding herself about the warning that her mother had given her in the very beginning that went like this: "if you can not forgive his infidelity baby girl then you better forget about getting married." DeShawn assured her mother that she could forgive and forget, and she did as long as Pa-Pa H came straight home every night.

FLY-DI 16
(THE HONEYMOON IS OVER)

DeShawn had another baby, wow! She gave birth to a beautiful little girl and once again that pregnancy was a breeze. She had the American Dream, one boy and one girl and the boy was the oldest, all she needed was the dog and white picket fence.

She was very happy playing the role of the dutiful wife and a loving mother to her children. The children were growing-, nicely all things considered with married life going pretty well. DeShawn realized that the children needed more space so she applied for NYC Housing and she was accepted.

DeShawn informed her landlord that she would be moving and Mr. O was very sad to see his tenants leave, she was pretty, sad too however, she knew that the kids needed space to play. All was well, eveything appeared to be falling right in place. There was only one problem DeShawn could hot forget that Pa-Pa H had been unfaithful.

She really thought that she could put it behind her, but it continued to come to the fore front of her mind everytime Pa-Pa H hung out with the so-called boys. Several years had passed and the pain was still there. Pa-Pa H was.the only man that DeShawn had knew and loved. She could not understand why he did what he did. She also wondered if Pa-Pa H would have married her if his play thing would not have come to light.

DeShawn went to sleep and woke up day after day, week after week, month after month with these issues around infidelity going through her mind, that's not good and she knew that! But she kept on going, she continued to bury her feelings deep down in her heart. She was very family orientated and her family was her all and all.

DeShawn knew how she felt inside, she kept reflecting back to the telephone call that she received from her now husband's ex-girl! The threat of Pa-Pa H being made to marry his ex and then after she gave birth to her child she would divorce him so DeShawn could have him just wouldn't go away. As time went on DeShawn became very angry with herself, she was reacting just like her mother did and she could not stand the thought of being like her mother when it came to her man.

DeShawn thought that she forgave Pa-Pa H however, she was very aware of the fact that she would never forget what he did to her. She was always true blue to Pa-Pa H, she even reflected back to the first time when she was intimate with Pa-Pa H and he had the nerve to say to her, "Oh, I did not know that you were a virgin." She recalled the pain that she felt when he made that then horrible statement. She felt as though Pa-Pa H could have kept those negative feelings to hisself. DeShawn felt like Pa-Pa H should have been hornored to have been given the liberty to have taken DeShawn's most precious jewel. As time went on the apartment was working out very well. The kids were now in school and she had become the dutiful wife, the loving mother and the PTA President.

DeShawn reflected back to her yester years when she was about 11 years old and her father came home with a red 3 wheeler bicycle that was not newt. DeShawn remember asking her father who the bike was for and her father went off on DeShawn telling her how ungrats£&j£, she was and how she should appreciate the fact that her god-father-had gotten the bike from one of the Jewish families that he used to work for, mind you DeShawn was 11 years old with a size 8 shoe and stood 5feet, 2 inches tall, funny! Grateful, don't make me laugh she said to herself. She remembered the Christmas in particular because she had gotten a brand new dress for that Christmas, no hand me downs. DeShawnfs mother had brought her a brand new royal blue dress. The dress was solid electric blue on the top in a valour material blue and white satin stripes on the bottom with a big red velvet bow in the back.

She really loved that dress and it was brand new! DeShawn's sister received the exact same dress for Christmas and that annoyed her for a little while however, it was not a hand me down. She was determined that her children would always have a very special Christmas. DeShawn really loved her children, her whole life was centered around her children and making sure that her children had all of the things that she did not have when she was growing up, even down to the nuclear family no matter what it took.

DeShawn suffered from a geat deal of issues, the three men that she loved, trusted, admired and adored caused her so much pain. Let's talk about DeShawn's brother! You already know about Pa-Pa H and her father, now her brother he was her all and all. DeShawn and her brother let's call him Swift, they were unseparable, they did everything together. When you saw one you saw the other. Swift taught DeShawn to play basketball, run track, shoot skellies and for heavens' sake don't leave out how to fight!

She could fight, she would fight at the drop of a dime. She was very aggressive and very angry and mean. DeShawn growing up always blamed her torn boy ways on her brother. Swift use to screen all of her boy friends. If he did not like them DeShawn could not talk to them. Swift allowed her to talk to one dude and that dude was one of his best friends.

DeShawn remembered hanging out with her brother and his best friend C.C., she really liked him however, he was not very affectionate, little did she know then that her brother allowed her to deal with C.C. but he warned C.C. if he had sex with her he would hurt him. DeShawn and her brother were like twins, she always used to think of herself as the brother that Swift always wished for because he was the only.boy surrounded by four sisters and he was next to the youngest, I think that's called the knee baby and DeShawn was the baby.

Yes, they did everything together. She remembered that her brother would never allow her to wear bras. He used to make her wear tee-shirts, DeShawn never dealt with her sisters on the girly tip. Everything was about her and her brother. She talked to her brother about eveything. DeShawn remembered the first day she entered womanhood. Her and her brother was out-side in front of their building playing, Swift was playing punch-ball and she was jumping rope when all of a sudden she felt wet between her legs, at first she thought that perhaps she might have urinated on herself, but she knew better than that.

DeShawn never forgot that day, she had on a pair of yellow paddle-pushers what we call todays' capris' and a white tee-shirt. She went over to her brother now mind you she had 3 sisters and her mother was right up stairs sitting in the window where she always sat when her kids were outside playing. She told her brother what was going on, she remembered him becoming very angry and he said to her, "Go up stairs and go in the bathroom and lock the door until I get back." DeShawn did what she was told, she went up stairs and went to the bathroom and locked the door until her knight in shining armour returned. She remembered him going in the bag and pulling out this purple box that read Kotex! Swift handed her a long white cotton looking pad and directed her to put it between her legs. She did as directed and he said, "OK, let's .go." There was never a word ever spoken about what DeShawn later.found out to be her period, her monthly, her visitor depending on who you spoke to about it.

DeShawn remembered the look on her mothers' face when she found out about 5 months later that DeShawn was getting her period and that her brother knew all the long; Blondie which was DeShawns' mother nick name was heated, they called her Blondie because of the color of her hair. That was the very first time DeShawn ever remembered her mother being so angry.

Yes, DeShawn and her brother was glued together like super glue. As time went on they began to grow into young adulthood.

As time would have it and as strange as it appeared Swift only dealt with DeShawns' friends. Swift was really in love with one of DeShawns' best friends and we are going to call her Bren. He really cared a great deal for her and then something happened, he knocked up DeShawns' other friend, let's call her Red. Now that was some deep dodo! Deep dodo because Swift was in love with Bren! Well Red decided that she was going to keep her baby. Surprisingly enough Bren decided to stay with Swift and they argued for a minute and everything continued as normal!

Then all hell broke loose, DeShawn thought that she was going to loose her cotton picking mind. Her brother, her comforter, her best friend was arrested for a murder he did not commit. DeShawn was devastated. She remembered when the police came to her mothers' house and her mother cried like a baby when they took her only son out her house for a murder she knew her son did not commit. DeShawn cried too. DeShawn remembered her mother asking her father for some money to obtain a lawyer for their son.

DeShawn remembered hearing her father say (quote, unquote) "No one in my family has ever been arrested and my son has messed up the familys' name and if he do not tell me what happen I am not going to waste my money." Well, I guess he did not hear what he wanted to hear and the next thing DeShawn knew was thai: her brother was going to jail and may never return.

DeShawns' heart was broken in two, her brother took a past of her heart with him. DeShawn was so very angry at her father and so was her mother. All the love that her mother always had for her husband left along with her respect for him when he allowed their only son to go to jail for something we knew he did not do. This was a rough time for DeShawn! DeShawn held her father at fault for not providing money for an attorney and allowing her brother to be represented by a Legal Aide, who might I add was paid by the city ha-ha, joke, joke, how much representation did he have? DeShawns' life was never the same, her brother took a piece of her heart and her world came tumbling down.

FLY-DI 17
(HUMPTY DUMPTY)

DeShawn finally realized how Humpty Dumpty felt when he sat on the wall and how he felt when he had his great fall and no matter what took place in DeShawns' world she could not put herself back together again. Yeah, she was definitely able to identify with Humpty Dumpty only this was real life and in technicolor.

DeShawns' world seem to come crashing down on her. All the men that she loved with all of her heart had abandoned her. Her husband with his infidelity which DeShawn could not forget, her father and his street life and now her brother, what next?

DeShawns' children was now in school full time and DeShawn had a great deal of time on her hands. Too much time to-think. Being the PTA President of her childrens' school suddenly was not enough. DeShawn felt like she was going to loose her.mind, so she decided that she was going to go back to school to obtain her G.E.D., that's right DeShawn was a high school drop out and a very fine mother and wife.

DeShawn was very proud of her motherhood and very grateful to her husband who could have abandoned her, but instead he married her. DeShawn needed something in her life to keep her from feeling the pain of her mother who missed her son dearly and for herself who could not control the anger that she felt for her father and the abandonment issues that she was feeling.

DeShawns' entire life appeared to be falling apart. DeShawn decided that she could not control anyone elses' ways, feelings or actions, but she could damn well control who comes into her life, who she allows to stay in her life and who she allows to leave her life and still be content.

Unlike Humpty Dumpty and all his Kings' Horses and all the Kings' Men couldn't put Humpty Dumpty back together again, poor Humpty.

DeShawn was not Humpty Dumpty and she decided to begin to put her life back together again piece by piece. So she went back to school, the kids were bigger, more independent and she could begin to do her thing! DeShawn took her G.E.D. for the very first time and determine to pass that test and she did. After taking and passing her G.E.D. DeShawn felt her independance returning. She had become motivated. Her pain of abandonment remained however, it did not hurt so bad.

DeShawns' husband was not very happy about her accomplishment and he even had the nerve to question her about why she wanted to attend school and attempt to become gainfully employed. Her accomplishments had become a threat to him. He felt as though he was loosing his control and he was because DeShawn was determine to become employable and to further her education.

Immediately after passing her G.E.D. DeShawn enrolled in college. She had become a mother, a house wife, a student and a employee. DeShawn remembered going down to what we called Welfare at that time with her boldness and tenacity and she informed the employees at the office that she did not want to apply for public assistance! DeShawn explained that she was . looking for employment. DeShawn remembered this afro-american lady at the front desk of the Welfare Center informing DeShawn that the office she was in was not a employment agency! DeShawn replied that she was well aware of her location and she also stated that she was not going to leave that office until someone assisted her with her needs. DeShawn went on to inform them that they should be grateful that she was not seeking monetary gain and in fact she was willing to work.

As the conversation continued and might I add it became heated at one point!

A Caucasian man came down the hall and introduced himself to DeShawn and asked could he help her? DeShawn replied, "Yes, you can!" She went on to explain to the man that she was well aware of the fact that she was in a Welfare Center and not an employment agencey, she also explained that she was not there to apply for public assistance however, she was seeking employment.

The man instructed DeShawn to follow him. The man began to inform her about this program called C.E.T.A. and he went on to assure her that it was right up her alley and just what she was looking for. The acronym C.E.T.A. meant Comprehensive Employment and Training Act, DeShawn was thrilled. That particular day was the first day of DeShawns' new beginning.

DeShawn landed a clerical job at a very prestigious organization about 30 minutes away from her house. What more could DeShawn ask for? The kids were growing up fast, time was not standing still. Pa-Pa H was not happy at all. DeShawn had become her own person. Life had turned completely around.

DeShawn began taking driving lessons, she was determine to pass that test just.as she passed all the other tests, written test, physical test and the emotional test. DeShawn had developed this positive attitude.. Everything that DeShawn had set out to do came to pass.

DeShawn failed her first driving test but she did not give up. She took the road test again and she passed with flying colors. A couple of weeks later DeShawn bought her first car, a used car I might add and she purchased the car from one of Pa-Pa H friends. The car ran very good, it had a nice body, the color was not that great but it got DeShawn from point A to point B. Pa-Pa H was really pissed off and by the way he could not drive nor did he have a drivers' license.

As time went on DeShawn was moving at her own pace and there was no stopping her now. The children were meeting her halfway and they were very proud of their mother. Now on the other hand Pa-Pa H was totally bent out of shape.

DeShawn no longer had the need to rely on him for everything and that was a no, no hum! DeShawn was doing very well in school and was passing all of her classes with B's and B+. DeShawn was so very proud of her accomplishments. Although DeShawn lived in Brooklyn and worked in Brooklyn her school was in Manhattan, 3 days a week DeShawn traveled back and forth from work to school.

She was so very proud of how her life had turned around and how the pain in her heart had eased up, oh don't get it twisted she continued to miss her brother however, it had become tolerable. Before DeShawn realized it 2 whole years had passed and she was halfway through her education.

DeShawn remembered walking toward her school one spring evening when she heard someone call her name. DeShawn turned around and she saw an old friend from the project who worked in the area and hung out in the bar that she was standing in front of after work. She invited DeShawn to stop by after school. DeShawn was so very glad to see her old friend Bee Bee. DeShawn gave Bee Bee her word that she would stop by one day after school. Bee Bee assured DeShawn that the bar was her hang out and that whenever DeShawn stopped by and she was not in the front of, the bar DeShawn should look in the bathroom for her because she definitely hung out in that bar.

FLY-DI 18
(FEELING LIKE CHAKA KAHN ONCE YOU GET STARTED IT'S HARD TO STOP)

DeShawn decided to meet Bee Bee at the neighborhood saloon after school. DeShawn never really hung out, she was really a home body person, mother and wife. The atmosphere in the spot appeared to be pretty cool. It wasn't too light and it wasn't too dark, it appeared to be just right. Everybody knew everybody in there or at least that's the way it appeared.

When DeShawn rolled up in the spot, fine as she was everybody turned around to catch a glimpse of that fine slim thing that had just walked through the door. DeShawn scanned the joint to see if she spotted'her long time friend or should I say associate!

DeShawn and Bee Bee never really hung out, Bee Bee was really associated with DeShawn's older sister. Anyhow, after DeShawn scanned the joint and did not catch a glimpse of her girl Bee Bee nor did she hear her loud hoarse voice, DeShawn began to make her exit towards the door not wanting to ask anyone for Bee Bee when she heard that hoarse voice say, "Yo DeShawn." DeShawn stopped dead in her tracks and made an about face, you see Bee Bee had a voice that was so different than any voice you have ever heard, if you were speaking to her over the telephone you would swear out right that you were speaking to a man. And it was on!

Bee Bee began bringing DeShawn up to speed on the joint. Bee Bee introduced DeShawn to everybody and their mother. Every person that she introduced DeShawn to she had a story that came with the person and the introduction. DeShawn remembered meeting one female who in particular did not sit well with her. The chick thought she was all that and then some and she checked DeShawn out from top to bottom.

Now remember, DeShawn was five feet six, weighing in at 140 lbs., size 9 dress and had big legs to go along with her dress and lets' not talk about the size of her butt, (smile) Now when they were giving out hips and breast DeShawn was at the end of the line so she missed out in those areas, but everything was in proportion and DeShawn looked 10 years younger than she really was.

The chicks were hating, but they kept it to themselves, and besides Bee Bee acted like she was the one and everyone appeared to flock around her like she was the man/woman. She controlled the bar and most of the situations that took place in the spot. Little did DeShawn know that once you got started it's hard to stop. Don't forget that DeShawn's marriage was really on the rocks because of the word unfaithfulness, a word that DeShawn just could not shake. No matter how hard DeShawn tried to shake her feelings of Pa-Pa H's infidelity and the fact that it was years later the feelings were by no means gone and forgotten.

DeShawn started hanging out at the bar. First it was only on her school nights, Tuesdays and Thursdays. Then it moved, to Tuesdays, Wednesdays, Thursdays and Fridays. Ya DeShawn was hanging out and she loved it. Hum payback was a mother. DeShawn's kids were always taken care of because DeShawn had an older daughter who took good care of her little sister.

Things started getting deep! DeShawn blended in with the in crowd very quickly. She had a very friendly personality .and made friends very quickly. Although DeShawn blended in she got along better with the dudes. Females either liked DeShawn or they didn't, there was no in between. DeShawn learned very quickly what hanging out in the bars was all about. She started getting high. It started off with the Budwisers and then she graduated to the Hennessey, now that took some doings. DeShawn always had a taste for beer but she had to develop a taste for the Hennessy, brandy for those who may not be aware of what Hennessy is.

Now remember DeShawn resided in the borough of Brooklyn and her school was located in Manhattan. Every week DeShawn drove from Manhattan to Brooklyn high as a kite and never received a ticket for DWI. In fact she never even knew what the letters DWI meant until much, much later, Driving While Intoxicated. Some days DeShawn was so twisted she did not even know how she got home in one piece.

DeShawn went from one get high to another. She became a master of get high and tolerance in the field of getting high. No one could have told DeShawn that she would be hanging out and getting high like a person who lost their cotton picking mind. DeShawn remembered her son telling her one day that yesterday was gone and that she will never be able to catch up or get back the yester years hum, great observation he made too bad DeShawn did not catch it.

She kept hanging out and partying, days turned into weeks, weeks turned into months and DeShawn did not care whether Monday fell on a Friday. DeShawn knew one thing for sure and that was no matter how much hanging out that she was doing she was going to graduate, not to .another drug, but to graduate from college and receive her. Bachelor's Degree in spite of!

Things continued to loolc up for DeShawn. She had already obtained a job working-for the city, her children were much older now and things were starting to come together, so DeShawn thought. DeShawn continued to do good in school. Her grades were no less than A .or B, she really worked hard to graduate with a good average. Little did DeShawn know that she was going to meet a knight in shining armor that she would fall head over heels for.

P.P. was fine as wine, oh yeah, he was all of that, he made you want to say, "hum, hum, good", ya that's right. Now you must remember that Pa-Pa H was the only man that DeShawn had ever loved, needless to say, she never was intimate with any man but Pa-Pa H. Thoughts of DeShawn being with another man intimately was out of the picture, then P.P. came along with his lean, fine self.

P.P. was a smooth talker, he spoke at a low tone and he smiled all of the time. DeShawn found herself showing up at the spot right after school and hoping P.P. would show up. P.P. used to work down the block from the spot that we hung out at. DeShawn started not caring whether Bee Bee showed up as long as P.P. showed up and when he did it was like heaven, wow like heaven, that's deep! When DeShawn conversated with P.P. he listened, he heard the things that she shared with him. He actually cared about people. He had a very loving and caring heart.

P.P. was so into family, he was a dedicated father however, he tried to be the loving paramour, the best that he could be. You see both P.P. and I had a lot in common. We both were in relationships that we did not want to be in, but we stayed in our individual relationships because of the children. See P.P. was grateful to his paramour for talking her parents into taking him in when his parents passed away and DeShawn was grateful to her husband for not abandoning her when they were younger and started their family. Pa-Pa H took care of DeShawn and their children. He made a home for them and DeShawn was very grateful for that. Remember DeShawn suffered from abandonment issues, issues around her father and her brother leaving her, the .loves of her life.

So as much as P.P. and DeShawn wanted to run off into the night and be together forever and ever, but they had an allegiance to their families and they could not imagine leaving their children and the place they called home even though their mates never knew of the holes in their souls and the lone-some-ness that they felt when they were at home having family night.

P.P. and DeShawn developed a relationship that was unreal. DeShawn never experienced anything like that before in her life. P.P. finished her sentences and always knew when something was wrong. Everything was so good with them. DeShawn continued to attend school and did very well I might add. The hanging out did not stop, the getting high did not stop and it had been going on for what seemed like a life time, traveling from one borough to another to attend school, and to hang out, talk junk, drink liquor, get high and look forward to the next day to repeat the behavior all over again. DeShawn and P.P. enjoyed what they shared when they spent time together. They were able to share their deepest darkest secrets. P.P. was so obligated to his paramour for saving his life and giving him a place to live and DeShawn had become uncertain as to what she was feeling and she started to wonder what payback felt like. DeShawn and P.P. made a promise to each other and the promise was, 'no matter how they felt about each other they would never come between each others' family', boy that was hard! Oh by the way they kept that promise.

Graduation was near and DeShawn knew that all good things had to come to an end. She thought about her graduation, not seeing P.P. anymore,, the constant thought of not seeing P.P. anymore was very hard for her. Although they were in total agreement of the seperation, DeShawn dealt with reoccurent abandonment issues once again. Every one she loves leaves her, why? DeShawn continued to get high, hang out only this time it was to get P.P. out of her heart, mind, body and soul. P.P. had become an intricate part of DeShawn's life and there was nothing she could do about it.

As much as DeShawn looked forward to graduating, graduating with a Bachelor's Degree, wow, that's really happening, DeShawn graduating with a Bachelor's with a 3.4 G.P.A. (grade point average) for those of you who are saying, 'what the hell is a G.P.A.', Oh I mean what the (hey smile!) DeShawn was very happy to be graduating however, graduating suddenly symbolized not being with.P.P. anymore so it kind of took the joy out of looking forward to graduating, but May was right around the corner. DeShawn continued to frequent the spot, talk junk, get high until the spot closed. In all of the hanging out and getting high DeShawn was able to pass her classes.

FLY-DI 19
(GRADUATION DAY)

The day finally arrived, Graduation Day. DeShawn was excited, ironically enough the thought of not seeing P.P. anymore for some reason did not even enter into DeShawn's thoughts. DeShawn was very proud of herself. She managed to graduate from college after acquiring a G.E.D.. Now you must remember DeShawn never really graduated from any school, she never attended her Jr. High School graduation, she just went on to her next grade, she thought she was too cool to attend the graduation, but little did she know that those days would come back to haunt her and they did!

Oh well, moving right along. It was graduation time,. DeShawn remembered thinking to herself oh wow, I made it. DeShawn had a determination in her spirit. Once she decided that she. was going to do something she would not stop until it was completed. DeShawn, had to prove to her father that in spite of her getting pregnant at an early age and marrying a St. Thomian instead of a Barbadian she was going to be somebody. DeShawn was determine to live life on her terms and not lifes' terms. DeShawn was determined to go as far as life would take her. DeShawn was determine never to settle for less, DeShawn wanted the finer things in life and that's it and that's all!

So the graduation ceremony began, DeShawn's mother was so proud of her baby. DeShawn's mother never gave up on her children in spite of all of their insanity, and God knows DeShawn had to be insane with some of the stuff she used to do. If I did not know better I would have thought that DeShawn had a death wish or something.

However, contrary to popular opinion DeShawn loved life and she adored her children. DeShawn's life was her children and she did not have to wonder where she learned how to love her children because all she had to do was look at her mother, she was an excellent role model.

DeShawn's family attended her graduation. DeShawn remembered this Caucasian woman who worked with her on her first city job. The woman was DeShawn's guardian Angel. DeShawn thought that she had to fight every battle and did not have a problem doing it, but this lady Jean taught DeShawn how to choose her battles, and low and behold her and husband traveled all the way to New Rochelle, New York to attend DeShawn's graduation, that was so nice and DeShawn learned a very valuable lesson that daye, DeShawn learned that she was not prejudice and that she could love everyone in spite of.

DeShawn introduced Jean and her husband to her family. DaShawn was very happy that everyone had showed up for her special day. The commencement was about to start. The announcement came over the PA system. Everyone was directed to take their assigned seats and the graduates were directed to line up at the back of the auditorium.

DeShawn had this frantic look on her face and no one knew why. DeShawn knew! She was searching the crowd for the face of her father. DeShawn was saying to herself, 'you mean to tell me that all of this hard work paid off and her dad was not there to share in her accomplishment'. DeShawn eyes' began to tear up, once again she began to deal with her abandonment issues.

DeShawn's graduation was very important to her, but most of all it was a very special day because DeShawn did it her way. She was determine to walk down the isle when sha heard her name called come hell or high water. As DeShawn lifted up her head she caught a glimpse from her peripheral vision, a man, a man that resembled her father, DeShawn pulse quickened, her heart began to skip a beat, sure enough, it was her dad, scanning the graduates for his child.

Their eyes met and they both smiled at one another with a smile that neither one would ever forget. DeShawn's graduation day and her father's presence was very important, this was the day that DeShawn planned to confront her father about his negative behavior toward her, and how he directed her to terminate her pregnancy or else! Hum, he had his damn nerve, and mind you, he never said or directed DeShawn's 3 sisters who had at least 2 or 3 babies apiece to terminate their pregnancies. Oh yeah, this was the day that DeShawn was going to deal with her father's behavior toward her, her mother and definitely his negative behavior towards DeShawn's only brother who she loved so dearly.

Remember he would not give DeShawn's mother any money to hire a lawyer for her brother and her brother winded up going to court with an 18B lawyer, (legal aide) and he received 25 to life! Oh now that's some deep dodo. Yeah, DeShawn really had to deal with that, the feelings that she was harboring were pretty deep inside her heart. Yes, graduation day was the day that DeShawn chose to air her feelings for once and for all.

Moving right along. The graduation had begun, the Star Spangle Banner was sung as they pledged allegiance to the flag, notice I said they. DeShawn did not pledge allegiance to no flag. I guess some folks would call her disrespectful, oh well.

As the graduates marched in the honored guest stood to their feet. Each guest searching out their sister, brother, mother, father, aunt or uncle. DeShawn caught the eye of her mother first, who was standing like a peacock. DeShawn's mother was so very proud of her baby. DeShawn was the first of her mother's children to graduate from college. DeShawn was' very anxious for her name to be called. DeShawn's last name was almost at the end of the alphabet.

As she looked around marveling at the fact that her name was being called for the 4th most amazing accomplishment of her life. As DeShawn strutted her stuff down the isle to receive her degree she turned to look behind her at her father with a look that made a statement that said, "I told you so, I knew I could do it and so did mommy".

This was a day that DeShawn would never forget. It seemed like it took them forever to call the rest of the graduates' names. DeShawn was very excited as well as determine;to finally give her father a piece of her mind. The graduates were all in the lobby receiving graduation gifts and taking pictures with their loved ones. DeShawn went over to Jean and her husband and thanked them so very much for attending her graduation and assured them that their presence at her graduation had made a positive impact on her, DeShawn hugged and kissed them, took a couple of pictures and then walked them to their car. Before they entered their car, they handed DeShawn a card and they again congratulated her with the biggest smiles on their faces. DeShawn was sure that Jean's husband had already gotten the 411 on her. DeShawn. thanked them again and they left.

DeShawn then' went back to the lobby to rejoin her family. On the way back to the lobby DeShawn was tossing around in her head, now I'm going to get him. DeShawn walked up to;her mother and the children and informed them that she had to speak to her dad for a second and they were alright with it.

DeShawn kind.of had an idea that her mother was aware of her thoughts. DeShawn was very glad that her father was not stupid enough to bring his paramour to her graduation and he was well aware that DeShawn's mother would be there. DeShawn and her father commenced to walk in the opposite direction from her mother and the children. When DeShawn was out of view from her mother and the children DeShawn did a Linda Blair kind of thing and stared her father dead ih his face and looked directly into his eyes and questioned, "Why did you ask me to kill my baby and not only did you direct me to kill my baby, but you gave me an ultimatum that if I did not terminate the pregnancy I had to move out your house?"

DeShawn told her dad that she needed an answer to that question and that she wanted an answer that day. DeShawn's father first attempted to apologize to DeShawn for any pain that he might have caused her. By this time DeShawn was crying a river.

DeShawn's fathers' explanation was that he had placed such high expectation on her. DeShawn's father went on to explain to her that he always looked at her as the child that was most likely to succeed and when DeShawn became pregnant it just broke his heart. DeShawn attempted to explain to her father that each one of her sisters had 2 and 3 babies apiece and that he never once gave them the direction that he gave her, "kill your baby or move out". Again DeShawn's father attempted to apologize and asked for forgiveness and told her how proud he was of her. DeShawn again looked deep into her father's eyes and said, "Daddy why didn't you give mommy the money that she needed to hire an attorney for my brother?" and his response to that question was, "Your brother disgraced the family name by getting arrested" and DeShawn looked at her father and replied, "No dad you disgraced the family name when you left my mother with 5 children and no way to feed them and she she had to take a baby sitting job to make ends meet after nanny traveled to Brooklyn every week-end with 4 and 5 bags of food and we had to meet her at the bus stop to help her carry them after she carried them all the way from Manhattan. No, you're the one that disgraced the family's name when you disappeared for weeks and weeks at a time, you're the one that violated the terms of the marriage, you broke the contract by bringing you chic to the house that we called home on the week-ends when you all played cards and my mother was the clean up woman. Yeah and you got the nerve to talk about the word disgrace!"

For the first time DeShawn was able to express to her father all of the feelings that was harbored deep down in the far part of her heart. DeShawn went as far as to diagnose her father's behavior and to explain to him why it was so easy for him to do the things that he did to his family. DeShawn told her father that he was a carbon copy of his father who gave up on his son which was him. DeShawn's father was his father's only son who kicked him to the curb at a very young age, history does repeat itself!

As tears continued to roll down DeShawn's face her father could only stand there and look at her like he was in some type of pain, excruciating pain, yeah I guess the truth hurts DeShawn thought to herself. That day was yes one of the best days of DeShawn's life, she finally got all that trash out of her system. DeShawn felt like she had lost about 20 pounds and to top it all off, or should I say, it was the icing on her cake, DeShawn's father never asked for forgiveness for the things he did and did not do. However, DeShawn remembered her father expressing his love for her and how proud he was of her.

DeShawn did not know how to take her father's sentiments because she was a grown woman with 3 children and she had never, never remembered hearing her father say, "I love you", DeShawn was in a state of shock and after the shock wore off a second later DeShawn replied with this statement, "Dad I wish you would have said those words to me many, many years ago", she stated that she was a full grown woman and that at this stage of the game his love for her didn't much matter. DeShawn went on to explain to her father that his inability to display and express his love for her as a child taught her how to love her children unconditionally. She also expressed to her father how his inability to put his family first taught her how to put her children first. DeShawn looked at her father with pity and disgust, her father hugged her and handed her a envelope and told her to enjoy her day and he walked away speechless. For the first time in DeShawn's life she felt as though she paid her father back for not helping her mother with attorney fees for her brother and it wasn't even done intentionally! DeShawn was just shooting from both barrels and it felt real good to her.

DeShawn's. mother and children appeared just as her father was leaving the scene, DeShawn's mother questioned DeShawn and inquired whether she was alright? DeShawn replied, "I'm just fine mommy!"

DeShawn and her family took a few more pictures, her mother and her children told her how proud they were of her and how much they loved her and they entered the car and started back to the city to have dinner and to continue to celebrate DeShawn's graduation.

Everything went well, all was good and DeShawn really enjoyed the dinner and the gifts that she received, DeShawn saved her father's card and Jean's card for last. Once again her father crapped on her again. DeShawn opened the card from her father first and then opened Jean's card. Well I don't have to tell you that DeShawn's father gave her two dollars pass lunch money and Jean gave her enough money to buy lunch for a month. Once again DeShawn's father played hisself.

FLY-DI 20
(THE DAY AFTER GRADUATION)

The day after graduation everything is back to normal. DeShawn could not wait to inform her job that she had graduated with her Bachelor's Degree. She had been working at her job for almost ten years. Each time a higher position opened up and DeShawn applied for it the answer was, "Oh if only you had a degree we would be more than glad to give it to you!"

Well DeShawn waited patiently for the Office Associates' position to become available. A year had passed since DeShawn graduated and a position for an Office Associate had finally opened up. DeShawn was certain in her mind that the position would be hers because the director had assured her that the next position that became available would definitely be hers.

DeShawn waited and waited for the director to call her into his office for an interview however, DeShawn convinced herself that she really did not need an interview because she . had been employed with this city agency for 10 years. DeShawn decided to wait for the position vacancy post to change and it sure did, however, DeShawn's name was not the name that was posted!

DeShawn could not believe that they had passed her over, again. The director who looked her in her eyes and expressed to her how valuable she was to the agency, her supervisor who assured DeShawn that she would certainly put in a good word for her. Well, when push came to shove they took care of their own if you know what I mean! DeShawn was furious, she had to confront the director, not so much the supervisor because DeShawn realized that she did not have any pull, but the big dog looked me in the eye and gave what he called his word, so much for his word.

DeShawn met with the director and he could not even look her in her eyes. He had the nerve to express to DeShawn that she was a mighty fine worker and the fact that she was punctual and that they could always count on her to get the job done. DeShawn remembered asking the director if she was so good at what she did why didn't she get the job? Till this day DeShawn never got an acceptable answer however, he did offer DeShawn a substitute teaching job right in the district in which she resided in.

The director knew in his mind, heart and soul that DeShawn was not going to remain on that job in a provisinal spot for another year adn DeShawn took him up on his offer. She was placed in a Junior High School right in the develpment that she lived in.

DeShawn was teaching Special Ed Reading, boy was it rough! These teenagers were very difficult to reach. Before you could teach them you first had to reach them. They came with labels such as, Mis 3, CRMD, etc., wow, now that was deep. DeShawn thought to herself that this job was offered to her because no one else wanted it. After being in the classroom with that the school referred to as misfits DeShawn began to see them as a challenge and not as challenged left behind teenagers who were most likely no abel to succeed.

Anything taht DeShawn attempted to do, whatever mission she was ever sent on there was never an half stepping. DeShawn was determine to save at least one person out of a class of 17 students. At first the mission seemed impossible! DeShawn realized if she wanted to make this work she had to change her game plan. For the first two semesters DeShawn treated her students with loving kindness then she realized that the students was taking her loving kindness for weakness.

The following semester DeShawn's entire attitude changed. There had to be a level of discipline displayed in order to get their attention and of cause you know there is always one tough guy out the group and it happened to be a female who was struggling with her identity and DeShawn decided to use her since she stepped up to the plate to challenge the teacher.

DeShawn remembered the look that this particular student gave her when she entered the class for the first time and introduced herself to the class. DeShawn knew right then that this particular "wanna be dude" was going to give her fever. DeShawn being raised in the hood received her look as a great big project but one that she was willing to give her all. She became DeShawn's pet project. DeShawn decided that she would make a positive example out of her.

Then there was another nasty mouth female that had the nerve to live right on the same block as DeShawn, as a matter of fact right across the court, one building away. This particular female was under the assumption that because we were neighbors that she would become a privilege character, but little did she know that the rod would not be spared for her either and the fact that she lived right across the court was definitely not a plus for her.

DeShawn began to take control of her class from a different prospective and it worked. DeShawn did not take any shorts. When the students realized that DeShawn was not going to allow them to give up on theirselves because everyone else from their parents all the way down to the administration did, DeShawn was not.

The class began to turn around, the class started doing homework, reading books, writing book reports, taking spelling tests and passing. They had become very eager to please themselves as well as the teacher. Grades changed and so did attitudes in a positive way.

Two years had passed and the students were doing well particularly T.W. and L.J. who incidently turned out to be 2 of the top students in the class along with one other young man. Teaching was good however, DeShawn later found out that teaching was not for her. After graduation DeShawn moved on to what she thought was bigger and better things. The students had done well and DeShawn was very happy. There were some students who remained stagnated by choice because the damage was so deep rooted it would have taken 'rotor rooter' to remove the pain and needless to say the administration could not understand the change.

FLY-DI 21
(BIGGER AND BETTER THINGS)

DeShawn began working for a private agency. Oh, private agencies paid more however, your job could last for years or it could last for weeks or months, that was the chance you took when you worked for a private agency. DeShawn landed a job in a Mother/Child program in Brooklyn. This was a home for young women and their children. DeShawn was the social worker and she worked well with the mothers and their babies, but still DeShawn felt like something was missing. DeShawn continued to do her very best because that is who she was. Everything had a place and everything had to be in its' place.

DeShawn taught the young women how to love and respect theirselves. She also taught them the meaning of the words <u>principals</u> and <u>morals</u>. Most of the young women that were housed in that program never had their mothers around to teach them anything. The young ladies mothers were drug addicted and could care less about principals and morals. The women had ..low self worth and most of them could care less whether Monday, fell on a Friday. However, they loved their children. They kept their children very close to them and they were some what very over protective.

Most of the mothers had desire to complete their high school education where as others could only think about getting their own apartment and not have anyone telling them what to do. Working at the Mother/Child programs was very hard work. It took DeShawn back to her life at her mother's house and giving birth to her wonderful son at age 18. The difference between DeShawn and those girls was that DeShawns' sons' father was a good provider although he was not faithful.

Once again DeShawn could identify with the feeling of abandonment, it was like de-ja vu. Once again determination set in, DeShawn made a vow to herself to do everything in her power for these young women and their children. DeShawn through out her life always demonstrated a care givers' mentality.

Through out the years that followed DeShawn went from what we now call ACS back then was called HRA, Human Resouce Administration, to another form of attempting to protect mothers and babies to another private agency in New York, New York were she counseled mothers who children were in foster care, and they were in recovery from drugs and alcohol. DeShawn had to convince the children that their mothers loved them and then turn around and convince the mothers that their kids forgave them for all of the abuse and neglect, not to mention all of the mental and physical pain they caused them.

DeShawn, once again completed her task at that foster care program and continued to move on to what she thought was moving on to bigger and better things. DeShawn then obtained a job with another foster care agency where she counseled mothers and their babies, DeShawn seemed to be geared or should I say that she was driven to mothers and their babies.

Now might I remind you that during all the years of DeShawns' employment and .attempts to repair families DeShawn continued to get high, hang out and did anything that she was big and bad enough to do, not to mention things that she shouldn't have done. DeShawn was not too sure of the statue of limitation on some things that was so deep and so far fetched that she realized that some things are better left unsaid!

DeShawn had finally gotten remarried and continued to save families lives by counseling and therapy. Yes, DeShawn had finally gotten over P.P., no not Pa-Pa H, he was gone, yes I said completely gone and so was P.P., you know P.P. the one that DeShawn was seeing while she was doing her undergraduate work.

Well DeShawn married a man that called hisself Hollywood, Hollywood was also in recovery, I told you DeShawn was always a care taker, even in her marriage. Hollywood obtained the name Hollywood because he used to dress real fly in his days. Hollywood was a very loving man however, he wasn't very strong. You see Hollywood was an old time drug addict who went away to a residential treatment program however, he attempted to change his ways and he did pretty good. The only problem Hollywood had was although he was in treatment, residential that is, his thoughts and heart did not change he loved that white lady and I'm not talking about DeShawn.

DeShawn could not figure out why she had a desire and I mean strong desire to help other people. DeShawn was almost driven to aid any and everyone that she could. DeShawn loved to put a smile on a person's face. DeShawn even went as far as to land a job in a woman's facility where she counseled young and old women about preparation for their return to society, behavior modification,relapse prevention and after care. DeShawn's nick name should have been Helping Hand instead of Fly Di, she was always there. DeShawn had her mothers' ways that's for sure. There was no doubt about where her loving kindness came from. DeShawn continued to hang out, drink liquor, smoke cigarettes and whatever else she chose to do hummmm, let's see how far your imagination can take you, yeah she did it all.

DeShawn never could understand how she was able to do such an effective job on any job that she was employed with. DeShawn took her job very serious in spite of how often she hung out, and no matter how high she may have gotten the week end before. DeShawn often wondered whether there was really such a thing called Functional Addict! A Functional Addict was a person that could get high as often as they did by choice and manage to keep everything in tact, well that was DeShawn.

Everyone around her, the partners that she hung out with lost their jobs, homes, their relationships and their children. Mostly everyone that DeShawn hung out with they all had very good jobs, teachers, accountants, etc.. DeShawn did not realize how lucky she was until one day on a Friday night her and her neighbor had hung out in DeShawn's house all night after the children went to sleep, that's right after the children went to sleep! See DeShawn could not get high alone, she always had to have someone around her, call it paranoia whatever, she could not get high by herself. So all the get high was gone and there was one Newport left and a half bottle of Budwiser what you'll now call a 40 oz., yeah it was like that!

DeShawn's partner was about to leave and DeShawn walked her to the door and watched her get in the elevator and then she watched from the window as she walked across the court to her building. By this time it was about 4 O'clock in the a.m., that's right 4:00 in the morning. DeShawn looked at the half bottle of beer and the one cigarette that was left, well DeShawn decided to finish that off and she did. As DeShawn sat in her room all alone, waiting for her friend to ring the phone insuring that she arrived safely to her destination. After the telephone rang and DeShawn spoke with her friend she said good night and then hung up. All of a sudden DeShawn found herself all alone. DeShawn never felt so lonely, her friend was gone, the drugs were gone, the booze was gone and so was the money. Yeah that's right, all the money that we spent to purchase what we thought we needed for our perfect evening of relaxation, yeah right.

DeShawn and her partner both were in denial. This private relaxation week-end had become a every week-end affair. This had been going on for what seemed like forever. DeShawn realized that all of that week-end hanging out needed to stop, the bars, the clubs and even her relationship with her husband who loved the white lady more than he loved her.

DeShawn knew that her life had to change. Yes, she continued to be gainfully employed, she remarried a man who loved her dearly and was very good to her however, she realized that there was no future with him. Although DeShawn continued to be employed and had some of the finer things in life, her project apartment resembled a mini penthouse, mirrors on the walls etc., but something continued to be missing in DeShawn's life. There was a void that she could not fill, something was missing and DeShawn could not figure out what it was.

She was no longer hanging out on the week-end with her home girl from around the way, but she continued to do her thing only this time she made money as oppose to spending money you know what I'm talking about 1 It was all good, however, that lonely feeling was still there and it had become a mystery to DeShawn. She could not figure out why the hole in her heart was so deep.

Even though DeShawn had brought a car and began to travel and continued to reside in the project after she had divorced her first husband Pa-Pa H there was something way down deep inside of her. Yes, DeShawn did suffer from abandonment issues however, the feelings that DeShawn was feeling had nothing to do with abandonment, there was an empty hole in DeShawn's heart and the clubs and bars was her escape, yeah she felt the need to escape quite often. She was well aware of the fact that a change was needed and she was in agreement that a change was needed, but where did she start.

The project life was not it, the second husband that loved the white lady was still there, but it was like he wasn't. DeShawn began suffering from chronic asthma, hospital stays and the whole nine, but none of that seemed to make a difference. She had asthma attack after asthma attack, hospitalization after hospitalization and DeShawn continued to do the usual, hang out! The moment that DeShawn was released from the hospital the clubbing and bar hopping continued.

If I didn't know any better I would think that DeShawn had a death wish, bam! wrong thought, DeShawn loved her children with all her heart there is no way in the hell DeShawn would want to die and leave her three children behind, remember she had three children, yes she did and she loved them all the same.

Time moved on, things changed and some things remained the same. DeShawn continued to be employed, continued to hang out. DeShawn remembered hanging out one week-end and she was up in the spot, yes her favorite spot and she was sitting at the bar in her usual spot doing her usual thing and all of a sudden she got a pain in her upper thigh, the pain was so severe she thought that she was going to loose her mind. DeShawn tried everything from soup to nuts to kill the pain, no can do! The rest of the evening was pure madness, the pain was devastating. DeShawn tried-anything, that's right anything and everything to stop the pain.

Morning came and DeShawn dragged herself to the hospital. She was informed by the doctor that she needed a hip replacement and she needed it ASAP. DeShawn of course sought out a second opinion and the results were the same. DeShawn decided that nothing could hurt anymore than the constant pain that she was always in. She decided to go ahead with the surgery. Having the surgery meant that she would be laid up for about six weeks and she would be flat on her back because the doctor informed DeShawn that both her hips needed to be replaced. DeShawn decided that she was not going to go back and forth and have two operations. She informed the doctor that if he could not do both hips at the same time then she was not going to do any. DeShawn knew if she did the one and it was painful she would not go back for the other one.

Well, the surgery was scheduled and DeShawn was very afraid. The week-end before the surgery DeShawn and her partner hung out one more time for the usual week-end hang out. DeShawn's oldest daughter was nine months pregnant and was going to deliver her baby any day, yes time sure flys when you're having fun.

So we hung out one more time and it was the same ritual all over again. We hung out until the wee hours in the morning, the cigarettes, the Budwiser beer and everything was gone. DeShawn once again walked her partner to the elevator, watched her walk across the court and then waited for the 'I'm home telephone' call.

Once again it was the wee hours in the morning and DeShawn was all alone, high as a Georgia pine feeling completely empty and all alone. DeShawn did her thing and her husband Hollywood did his thing and then they would come back together. Hollywood always denied that he relapsed, but DeShawn knew better, old habits die hard.

So it's now Sunday morning about 9:00 a.m., DeShawn is unable to sleep she had been tossing and turning when all of a sudden a voice from no where came to her and .it spoke these words, "Get up, wash your face and go to churchl" DeShawn thought that she was bugging out. DeShawn looked around and no one was present. DeShawn laid back down and tried to go to sleep, but could not. The voice once again said, "Get up, .wash your face and go to church!"

DeShawn began to speak back out loud and the conversation went something like this: "I don't know what church to go to, where should I go?" The word came again, "Get up, wash your face and go to church." Defiant as DeShawn always was she got up, washed her face and brushed her teeth. Little did she know that brushing her teeth would only make the smell of the beer she drank all night permeate. However, DeShawn got dress and walked toward the back of the project where she found a church dead in the middle of the project and the service had just begun.

DeShawn walked into the church still tweeded, she remembered a evil usher walking up to her and asking DeShawn what was she doing there. The usher had a funky attitude, her demeanor was definitely not Christ like at all. DeShawn's reply was as follows: "I don't know what I'm doing here, but one thing I know for sure is that I am not leaving here!" The usher looked at DeShawn like she had four heads and she directed DeShawn to a seat in the back.

DeShawn paid her direction no mind and DeShawn walked up front and sat in the forth row. The service was pumping, the choir sang out the depths of their hearts. DeShawn began toget into the service, she began clapping her hands and getting into the service. DeShawn watched all of the members as they clapped their hands and stomped their feet. DeShawn joined in and little did she know that she was hooked. The high she felt that day was better than any high that she had ever felt and guess what, the high was free of charge.

FLY-DI 22
(THE BEST WAS YET TO COME)

DeShawn continued to attend church, she went to morning service, afternoon service, bible study and the whole nine. DeShawn took notes at bible study and became a great prayer warrior! DeShawn became hungry for the lord. All she could think of was the lord and going to church.

Months had passed and DeShawn continued to trust God. Well one day DeShawn rain into her home girl, yeah the partner from around the way and all hell broke loose, DeShawn and her partner did an over nighter, see DeShawn was serving God and her partner wasn't. After that one night DeShawn started clubbing again, the ripping, the running, yes today we call it relapsing, back then it was called oops!

DeShawn continued to hang out, she knew what she was doing was outside the will of God. DeShawn also knew her scriptures because she hid them in her heart and one thing she knew for sure that the scriptures' stated that 'who the.son set free is free indeed', if you don't believe DeShawn check out John 8:36. DeShawn knew once God placed his hands on you he would not let you go! DeShawn knew that if she continued to rip and run the streets the end results would not be good. DeShawn loved her children with the love that Jesus had for her. She knew that if she looked toward the hills from which her help comes from she would be fine. DeShawn remembered how severe the pain was in her hips and how it constantly kept her at someone elses' mercy because walking had become very difficult. DeShawn was very independant and her hips kept her very needy so she had her hip surgery and she did it her way, she had both hips done at the same time.

During her stay at the hospital her daughter gave birth to her first child and DeShawn was not there to see such a great miracle! A miracle the doctors said would never take place, you see the doctors told DeShawns' daughter that she would never be a mother, but little did they know, DeShawns' daughters' determination was very strong and she gave birth to a beautiful little girl who became her life just as she was DeShawns' life.

DeShawn continued to recover from her surgery and the birth of her second grandchild was enough to heal her almost instantly. During DeShawns' surgery she was only able to sleep on her back. She could-not move to the left nor could she move to the right, the only thing that she could do was look up! DeShawn began to talk to God about her life and the changes that she knew was needed. DeShawn refused to make God any promises and especially promises that she might not be able to keepi DeShawn continued to lay flat on her back looking up towards the author and the finisher of her life. DeShawn prayed and asked God to continue to heal her body. She remembered that her God was able to do exceedingly abundantly above all that she ask or think according to the power that worketh in us, Ephesinas 2:20 and that is what DeShawn relied on when she prayed for healing.

Healing came for DeShawn and she was discharged from the hospital. All was good she continued to pray and worship God. She prayed that her hips would heal and that she would not have to wear one big shoe with a lift and one regular shoe, you know DeShawn was very vain! DeShawn went from a walker, yeah that's what I said, a walker to loft stand crutches to regular crutches to a cane. DeShawns' rehabilitation went well and no she did have to wear a lift on her shoe thank God!

DeShawn was able to assist with her new granddaughter. Yes, things were starting to look up. DeShawn was able to go back to church and this time when she started she was determined to go all the way.

DeShawn attended church like a bandit, she never missed a beat, whatever was going on in the church DeShawn was there before the church doors opened up. She started bible study and took them very seriously.

Well, it was a year later and DeShawn was baptized! She remembered the day that she decided to be baptized. DeShawn was very afraid, she was always afraid of water and although it had been one year since the hip surgery she was afraid that the deacons would drop her and she would either drown or injure her hips. The deacons began singing this song that went something like this, 'Wade in the water, Wade in the water children, Wade in the water, God's gonna trouble the water'. After the last chorus of 'God's gonna trouble the water', they dunked DeShawn in the water and DeShawn went under. They immerged DeShawn for what seemed to DeShawn like an hour however, it was only long enough to say, "In the name of the Father, Son and Holy Ghost", DeShawn came up crying and praising God and it was on.

DeShawn remained in that church worshiping.and working on the battle field for her lord. DeShawn loved praising Godl She also knew that God was going to do a new thing in her life. DeShawn continued to praise God and she also charged God to his word. John 14:14, If I shall ask anything in his name, he will do it. Well DeShawn began praying that her family would get saved. DeShawn was growing in the word and the lord was using her mightily. She began to feel like the church that she was attending was not feeding her the meat. She felt like the church continued to keep her on breast milk, DeShawn needed more. DeShawn could not put her finger on the emptiness that she was feeling in her spirit, but she knew that it wasn't happening for her any longer in that church. Maybe it was because the pastor and the deacons were seasoned or should I say old! The praise and worship was dry, it had no beat, DeShawn needed more.

So she left that church never seeking God's face for direction and she landed up going back to the church that she attended as a child, the church that her mother made sure that her and sibling attended every Sunday morning and after they went home after the morning service and had lunch they returned back to church for the afternoon service. However, DeShawns' mother never went with them, but her mother definitely knew the lord and she was a praying woman.

DeShawn continued to attend church every Sunday, it was all good because Hollywood started attending church with DeShawn, he would read the word with her and attend church with her every Sunday. DeShawn and Hollywood were married in the same church, the church

DeShawn grew up in. DeShawn made such a beautiful bride. Everything was so beautiful. DeShawn was so very happy. Her husband continued to attend church and study the word with her. The scripture that he did not understand he would seek clarity from DeShawn. DeShawn was at a place in her life where things were going well. DeShawn continued to pray and worship God. DeShawn remembered one Sunday she was all dressed up in her Sunday go to meeting duds and her brand new shoes. As she started to step into the elevator she realized that the people who hung out the night before had used the elevator for their public bathroom. This was constant, every week-end. DeShawn began speaking things as though they were because that's what her bible told her she could.

She began claiming a house, a brand new house far away from the project. DeShawn even went as far as to buy moving boxes and stored them in her apartment. DeShawn continued to fast and pray and she believed that God would answer her prayers and that he would give her the desires of her heart and he did just that. It took looking at eight houses, Yes I said eight houses and eight disappointments. DeShawn never gave up, she continued to pray and continued to speak those things as though they were.

The realtor reminded DeShawn that the real estate was a multi listing and from past experience might I add eight times and each time the house that DeShawn wanted was always gone by the time they returned back to the office to do the paper work. Well, something told DeShawn to go out to the office in all of that rain to see what was so important, and mind you DeShawn did not have a clue on how to get to Queens. Little did she know that God would be her pilot and that she would arrive at the office that she needed to be just at the right time, 'Go head Holy Ghost!'

DeShawn arrive at the office and the realtor took her out to a house in Queens to look at, remember DeShawn had no intentions on living in Queens because her entire family resided Brooklyn. DeShawn went out to look at the house, she remembered saying to God, "Lord let your will be done". It was in the late part of November as a matter of fact it was 2 weeks before Thanksgiving.

DeShawn arrived at the house, she remembered looking up and down the block before entering the house. The house had a very peculiar odor however, as cold as it was outside with the rain and all it was very very warm in the house and the house had not been occupied for over 2 years. DeShawn walked through the house, upstairs, downstairs and was .very pleased with the house, the kitchen was very small but DeShawn knew that she could make the kitchen do.

Prior to looking for and purchasing the house, DeShawn had lost her oldest daughter to an untimely death. DeShawn thought that she was going to lose her cotton pickin' mind. DeShawn's daughter was her best friend. DeShawn and her daughter was thick as thieves, they were cool and the gang! When her daughter met her demise DeShawn took her death very hard. You see her and her daughter use to always talk about purchasing a mother daughter house. Her daughter never wanted to raise her daughter in the project. When DeShawn's daughter met her demise if it had not been for the lord on DeShawn's side she could not imagine where she would be.

The only consolation DeShawn had in her daughter's death was that her daughter was saved, she sang in the choir and she was on the pastor's Aid Committee so DeShawn knew that her child was not gone, but in fact she had just moved on and that she was now working in the

Kingdom for the lord. So now you can understand the determination in why it was so important for DeShawn to find a house for her and her daughter's child.

The day finally came, the house was DeShawn's and the lord blessed them with a roomy 4 bedroom house, 2 bathrooms, a large living room and a formal dining room on a quiet block a half-block from the bus stop that took you to the train station. What more could we ask for.

FLY-DI 23
(Moving On Up)

We moved into our new house, we had Thanksgiving dinner on the floor in our house and we certainly had a lot to give thanks for. Yes, DeShawn took her husband Hollywood with her however, that did not last long. DeShawn realizes' you can run a horse until he is dead tired and then lead him-to water, but if he does not want to drink, come hell or high water he ain't gonna drink and Wood was like that sorry horse", he did not want to leave that white lady alone (the get high). DeShawn realized that he had become a hindrance he did not want anything out of life. No, he had no vision, he could not see pass the nose on his face, nose, hum, white lady, yeah that's right that's all he could see and that was the desires of his heart. Some where deep down in his heart DeShawn knew he loved her howevar, as Tina Turner stated, "What's Love Got To Do With It!"

Love could not pay no mortgage so DeShawn had to cut that jigger loose. DeShawn had her priorities together, she was not afraid to step out on faith. DeShawn was aware of the fact that faith is a leap in the dark with a sure landing, DeShawn took that leap and all was well! DeShawn began to seek God's face in everything that she did. Things began to fall in place. DeShawn had gotten a new job and was doing what she does best, helping people. DeShawn was employed in a woman's prison as a drug counselor. It was there that DeShawn had met a man who professed to love the lord. DeShawn was definitely not looking for a man because frankly she had had enough of the sorry behind men who claimed to be proud of DeShawn's progress and her achievements. You know some black men claim to appreciate aggressive black women, hum, I beg to differ!

DeShawn enjoyed her job and the work that she was doing. DeShawn knew that she would not be on that job for the duration. She knew that that job was just her next stepping stone. DeShawn knew that she had to go back to school, she needed to further her education to begin to make longer money because she was now a home owner.

DeShawn- took yet another leap of faith and enrolled in a private college in Brooklyn. DeShawn was determined to achieve at the Master's level. DeShawn did not want to just attend the school and just pass her classes, DeShawn was going to work as hard as she had to work to graduate with a great, yes, I said great not just good Grade Point Average and her GPA was off the chain, I mean good. DeShawn was moving on up, she graduated from L.I.U., Long Island University which is a private institution with a Master's Degree in Guidance and Counseling.

If no one else was proud of DeShawn, DeShawn was very proud of herself and the progress that she had made. DeShawn continued to attend church, God continued to use her royally. DeShawn became a licensed minister. Yeah, DeShawn was moving on up! The man, the man that she met in the prison, no he was not incarcerated, the jail was a women's prison, remember! He was a CO., Correction Officer.

Yeah, we hooked up, he was very smart, very intelligent and had traveled all over the world due to his military background. DeShawn and G-man complimented each other in the beginning. All was good however, you never really know someone until you live with them. Now remember, DeShawn was saved! G-man wasn't saved but he knew the word and he loved the lord. DeShawn was quite sure of the fact that they could not live together because they were not married. So it was decided that DeShawn would rent out her basement apartment to Mr. G-man. The agreement was a good idea because it would save G-man some money and DeShawn too. By the way, it was G-man and DeShawn's co-worker who encouraged her to write this book.

G-man used to allow DeShawn the space that she needed to talk about her trials and tribulations without feeling condemned. Yes, G-man knew all about DeShawn's life and times and he not seem to care where she had been or where she came from. Although G-man loved who DeShawn had turned out to be G-man had some issues of his own. G-man had a love for alcohol. He was definitely what you would call a functional alcoholic! That was definitely his thing.

G-man knew the bible, he could quote you scripture and tell you the history of the black churches. Yes, he went to church every Sunday and became a deacon and if I must say so he was a mighty fine deacon. He was baptized almost immediately and performed his duties well. Little by little he' took on more and more responsibilities, he even taught Sunday School. DeShawn was very happy that G-man seemed to be very happy working for the lord however he continued to drink suds and smoke his cigaretts.

G-man began to see and realize that DeShawn really loved the lord! DeShawn was committed to her God, her church and her new way of life. DeShawn's entire life revolved around how she could serve the lord to the fullest. G-man continued to express his love for the lord and the church however, he was able to continue to hang out and do his thing. He felt like there was nothing wrong with a little bump and grind. In reality G-man and DeShawn's lives were so very different. DeShawn continued to study the word because the bible states' that we should study to show thy self approved unto God, a work-man needeth not be a shame being able to rightly divide the word of truth, 2 Timothy 2:15.

Little did DeShawn know that the lord was preparing her for the next phase of her life. Doors had opened up for DeShawn and she had been reached on a list that she was on for a position in law enforcement. DeShawn kept the appointment that she had received in the mail that directed her to report to downtown Manhattan for an interview. I don't have to tell you that DeShawn aced that interview and was appointed to the position.

Being appointed to the position meant that she had to put in her resignation at the women's prison and in doing that she had to seperate herself from the inmates who had developed a working relationship with her. Yes, leaving was not easy for DeShawn. I know you remember that DeShawn had experienced a great deal of abandonment issues in her youth and she could definitely identify with the abandonment issues that the inmates were feeling when they were informed that DeShawn had resigned and the reason for the resignation. Most of the inmates were very happy for DeShawn however, there were a few that harbored great resentment.

But the.beat goes on. G-man was elated that DeShawn had resigned because he no longer had to remind the gay women in the facility that I was his girl and they better stop drooling over her. All in all things went well and DeShawn's departure was made easy and G-man was happier than a pig in slop because he no longer had to worry about DeShawn getting hurt in the facility or getting caught up in a riot or something. That was always one of G-man's biggest concerns.

DeShawn was excited about starting her new job. DeShawn loved challenges 1 DeShawn went to church that following Sunday and gave testimony about how good God is to her and how God was just opening doors and giving her the desires of her heart. DeShawn remembered reading the bible and the promise that God made to her when he said that no good thing would be withheld from those who walk upright before Him and DeShawn knew that she was walking the walk and talking the talk so the promise was definitely hers. DeShawn started her new job and all was well, her new job took her back to the borough of Brooklyn.

DeShawn being employed in Brooklyn was convenient for her because it made it easier for her to visit her mother in the nursing home which was also located in Brooklyn. DeShawn's mother had suffered a heart attack 2 years prior which left her in a coma.

You see during the heart attack DeShawn mother's heart had stop beating for 15 minutes however, they brought her back to life which left her in a coma because she was not getting any oxygen to her brain which left her in a comatose state. DeShawn would go to the nursing home 2 days a week to comb her hair and to make certain that she was being taken care of and she was. DeShawn seeing her mother in that state really broke her heart, DeShawn hated seeing her mother like that.

DeShawn had been working at her new job for approximately 5 months when one day as she was sitting in her office as her co-workers prepared to attend a co-worker's funeral; DeShawn's intentions was to remain behind to cover the phones while the others went to the funeral. DeShawn stayed behind because she really was not that familiar with the co-worker that met his demise by his own hand, yeah that's right he took his own life, that's deep.

Suddenly DeShawn's telephone rang and the voice on the other end asked to speak to DeShawn, DeShawn replied,"This is she" and the voice on the other end said, "We lost your mother!" DeShawn replied, "What do you mean you lost my mother?" The voice repeated, "I'm sorry we lost your mother." DeShawn replied, "Well, where ever you lost her at you better go back and find her!" The voice then said, "DeShawn I'm sorry your mother passed away."

DeShawn remembered screaming to the top of her lungs, "OH NO, OH NO, OH NO!". DeShawn remembered beating on her desk saying, "Oh No, I just visited with her yesterday, she can't be, she can't be!" Mean while DeShawn's co-workers came running into her office. She remembered one of her co-workers in particular rapping her arms around her and whispering in her ear, "Weeping may endure for a night but joy comes in the morning!"

DeShawn was numb! Her mother, her best friend, her teacher was gone. DeShawn remembered saying to herself, "What will I do without my mother?"

DeShawn cried uncontrollably. DeShawn remembered her supervisor asking her if there was anyone she could call to come and get her? DeShawn replied, "No, I will be alright!"

DeShawn called the nursing home and directed them not to touch her mother and to leave her in the same position that she died in, the nursing home agreed. DeShawn regained her composure and thanked her co-workers and her supervisor for their blessings and she left. DeShawn's supervisor kept suggesting that DeShawn not leave alone but DeShawn assured them that she would be just fine.

DeShawn is a trooper or at least that's how it appears. DeShawn remembered calling her nephew and picking him up and heading toward DeShawn's.sister's job. When DeShawn arrived at her sister's job she rememebered asking for her sister's boss and informing him of the situation first. When he summoned DeShawn's sister and she observed DeShawn and her son walking toward her down the hall, she stopped and grabbed both sides of her face and began to cry.

Her first statement was, "What happened' to mommy? you never come to my job, what happened to mommy? she dead isn't she? she died right?" DeShawn began hugging her sister and trying to comfort her sister, but at the same time she needed comforting herself.

DeShawn remembered saying to her sister, "I know you think that you are not as strong as me however, today I need you to be strong for me!" DeShawn's sister looked at her baby sister and said, "I don't know if I can!" DeShawn remembered saying to herself, "Damn, (and you know that damn is not a curse because beavers build dams) not again, where is my big sister when I need her?" In case you forgot DeShawn was the youngest of five children. DeShawn's oldest sister and middle sister had already met their demise in their early years, and remember DeShawn's brother was doing twenty-five to life, that's right, that's what I said, for a crime that he did not even commit, a crime that he swore to DeShawn on their mothers' respirator before her demise that he did not do it.

DeShawn knew that her brother would never lie to her about anything and DeShawn believed in her brother, so not only did she have to be strong for her sister she also had to be strong for her brother too. Well, what about DeShawn? who was going to hold her down? I mean be there for her?

DeShawn knew that her job was cut out for her, the only thing that kept DeShawn strong was the fact that she was aware that she served a God that would not lie, she was well aware of the fact that her God sat High and He sees' Low.

DeShawn began to comfort her big sister who by the way was also saved, but at that time it was very hard to tell who was saved and who was the eldest. The fact that DeShawn had to hold it down, I mean take care of everything was alright because DeShawn's mother knew that she could handle it. DeShawn reminded her sister about Gods' promises in the word. DeShawn quoted one of her favorite scriptures to her sister from the Book of John chapter 14 verses 1 thru 3, "Let not your heart be troubled, ye believe in God, believe also in Me.: In my Father's house are many mansions if it were not so I would have told you." It goes on to say, "I go to prepare a place for you, I will come again and receive you unto myself, that where I am, there ye may be also."

DeShawn held tight to that word because she knew her mother was in her mansion, she also knew that her mother was laughing and sharing old time stories with her grand daughter. DeShawn's sister perked up a little bit after hearing that word, Hallelujah!

DeShawn, her sister and her nephew left her sister's job after thanking everyone for their love and understanding. On the way home in the car it was very quiet, there was so much to be said however, there was nothing said. DeShawn wanted to cry but for some reason she was unable to let it flow. DeShawn's sister cried just a little and she kept her eyes on her little sister and kept repeating the same question to DeShawn, "Are you alright?" DeShawn replied, "No, but I will be alright."

DeShawn called the family and they all met at DeShawn's mothers' house in the good old housing project that DeShawn grew up in. In returning back to her mothers' apartment sure stirred up some real serious unpleasant memories.

DeShawn called her father to inform him that her mom had met her demise. The family came together to plan the going home service for the great woman who was the thread that held the family together, Mama! She was the strongest black woman that DeShawn had ever had the pleasure of knowing. DeShawn remembered how her mother always encouraged her with positive afffirmations long before Maya Angelou wrote her first book of positive affirmations to the people of color!

DeShawn's mother used to always remind DeShawn of how important it was to never allow anyone to change your principals and morals she warned that if you allowed someone to change your principals and morals they are no longer yours!

DeShawn's mother always encouraged DeShawn by letting her know that she.could be whatever, she wanted to be and she always reminded DeShawn if she gives her word it's very important that she keeps her word and she always reminded DeShawn that her word was the only thing beside her education that no one would ever be able to take from her and those values stuck in DeShawn's head and in her heart.

FLY-DI 24

The pain that came after switching lanes, DeShawn had to bury her mother, play her favorite song, 'Precious Lord', write her obituary, pick her dress, find her a wig, pick her casket and make sure that all was well. The only cjlue that DeShawn had that kept her together was the word of God. DeShawn knew how to draw near to the Lord when things got rough. DeShawn by this time had learned to trust and depend on God completely.

It was such a wonderful feeling for DeShawn to remember how happy her mother was when she found out that her little big mouth hell raiser had became a preacher. DeShawns' mother used to pray for DeShawn all the time. It was the prayers of the righteous that availed and DeShawn thanked God for having a praying mother!

The funeral was very emotional. There was so many people in attendance, young and old. Everyone spoke so highly of DeShawns' mother, better known as Mama Syl or Gram. She looked so beautiful and peaceful. It appeared as though she had a little smile on her face and the preacher preached such a powerful message. There was no question in DeShawns' mind that everyone loved her mother. DeShawns' father took his wifes' death very hard because he never got a chance to apologize for all the pain that he had caused her and he now had to live with that.

Remember, DeShawns' mother was in a coma for 2 years before she met her demise. The funeral was over and the burial was the next day. Everyone came to the burial to pay their final respects to DeShawns' mother as well as the family. Boy let me tell you the burial was rough, everyone lost it when the casket went down in the ground. When they lowered the body into the ground DeShawn realized exactly what was meant by 6 feet under, the grave was deep, dark and cold.

DeShawn held on to the fact that the death of her mother only meant that she was absent from the body but present with the Lord and that was good. After the burial they all went back to DeShawn's mothers' house where they ate and shared 'remember when stories'. DeShawn was at peace with her mothers' death because DeShawn was well aware that her mother was very proud of who she had turned out to be. She had graduated with a Master Degree, she was not hanging out and getting high, she was actually a bonafided preacher, yeah DeShawns' mother was very proud of her.

Now on the other side of the coin DeShawns' brother took his mothers' death very hard. Although the facility transported him down to the funeral and he was allowed to socialize with the family he was not allowed to go out to the burial, yes that was rough! DeShawn thought her brother was going to lose his mind, but he held his head! DeShawn knew that her brother, her pal, her friend was hurting and there was nothing she could do about his pain! One thing was certain and that was DeShawns' brother loved his mother and he knew that his mother truly loved him unconditionally. DeShawn used the tool that she knew best to help her deal with the pain that she knew was devastating her brother, prayer, that's all she knew, it always worked for her in her deepest , darkest pain and challenges' prayer worked everytime. It was like food for the soul or should I say food to a hungry man!

Well now, the funeral and the burial was over and it was time to let the healing begin. DeShawn went back to work the next week and attempted to put her life back together. DeShawn had to come to the realization that her mama was dead, buried and gone from this life. Although DeShawns' mother had met her demise here on earth DeShawn was comforted by the fact that her mother was not gone she had just moved on! She was moving on up to a delux apartment in the sky and that was no lie, she had a place in the heavens of the heavens because DeShawns' mother was a sweet, loving, caring and giving woman who loved the Lord.

DeShawn began to make the adjustment on her now job. She met new friends and she learned an entirely new job which required a great deal of writing and concentration. DeShawn went right back to the same office that she had received the horrible phone call informing her of her mothers' demise. At first it was very difficult, a day wouldn't go by without DeShawn thinking of her mother. DeShawns' thoughts of her mother did not interfere with her productivity because the thought of her mother were good. Day after day DeShawn attempted to master the operations of her job. Week after week, month after month DeShawn did her thing!

Before we knew it, it was a year later. DeShawn continued to progress and time was not standing still for no one. DeShawn had a awesome supervisor and by having such an awesome supervisor it made learning the job easier. Everyday DeShawn became more and more independent, the lost of her mama and the pain had subsided. DeShawn was making more money than she was making on her last job, she had good medical coverage, what more could she ask for! Things were going great, DeShawn loved her job, she loved the Lord, she loved her beautiful house, she had it all. DeShawn drove from Queens to Brooklyn everyday to her place of employment, thank God for a reliable car, it got her to and from.

Time continued not to stand still. It is now 2 years since DeShawn had lost her mother, no let me change that, because DeShawns' mother was definitely not lost and we knew exactly where she was, so let me say since DeShawns' mother went to claim her mansion in the sky.

By now DeShawn was completely confident with her skills and her ability to write good reports, supervise a caseload of 150 high-risk and high profile individuals. DeShawn conducted cognitive counseling, made referrals for drug testing and treatment, mental health, domestic violence, educational and vocational training programs, corresponding with rehabilitation programs and maintained pertinent case records.

Yeah DeShawn was making it happen! DeShawn was good at what she did because she loved what she did. She loved working with people and took great pride in her work? but I guess you could say that there was still some who thought that she was very anal. Everything had to be just right, she took no short cuts and she took no shorts. She was very strong in her convictions and she never gave up on trying to get the individuals to see the good and to offer them clearer lens to see who they could become. DeShawn reminded the individuals that they must remain focused, confident and never to let anyone adjust their principals, because if they did then they were no longer their own principals because they have been adjusted by someone else.

It was early in the morning and as usual DeShawn was sitting in her office having her breakfast working on her report when the telephone rang, suddenly the strangest feeling came over her, a feeling of deja vu, she immediately recognized the voice on the other end of the line however, the voice was a voice of panic, it was DeShawn's nephew and he screamed, "DeShawn meet us at the hospital, Ta's been shot!" Shivering to shake herself of the shock DeShawn said shakily, "What? oh no don't tell me that, I don't want to hear that, no not again, it can't be, no, please don't tell me that! What hospital are you all at? what happened? who shot him?" Ta was DeShawn's first born, only son, the love of her life. DeShawn remembered thinking about how she had lost her daughter to a horrific gunshot death and now her son, oh no.

DeShawn arrived at St. Vincent's hospital in lower downtown Manhattan. She remembered pulling up in her car to the front of the hospital where she observed her family members standing outside. The family members that smoked were smoking as the others raced over to the car. DeShawn recalled getting out of the car shouting, "Who shot my baby? is my baby dead? who shot my baby? did Dred shoot my baby?" DeShawn's nephew pulled her to the side and said, "Aunty, you're not going to believe who shot Ta."

DeShawn replied, "I know Dred shot my baby, he was always jealous of my baby, I know he did it!" But her nephew said, "Calm down Aunty, it was not Dred, it was Tee." DeShawn became unglued, she began saying, "Oh no, he could not have done that, that was Ta's friend, he trusted him, they were road dogs, no that's not true." Her nephew Ka replied, "Aunty, jealousy is a hell of a thing!" But DeShawn just continued to say as if she was in a trance, "But why Ka? why? Ta would have done anything for that brother, he was like a brother to him and his mother was Grams' best friend." Ka replied, "He did it Aunty." That was when she lost all controllability and the tears began to roll down her cheeks as she said, "Take me to my baby, where is my baby, I want to see my baby." Ka simply stated, "You can't Aunty, you can't see him now he's in surgery."

DeShawn began to walk down the block she told her nephew that she would be alright, she just needed to be alone. As she walked away she began to summon itine Lord. DeShawn gave God back every word he had ever given to her. She reminded God that every good and perfect gift comes from above, she declared that her son would live and not die and declared the works of the Lord. She told God that He told her that He could do exceedingly and abundantly above all that we can ask or imagine, He said, "We have not because we ask not" and DeShawn asked God to spare her only son's life!

Days went by, weeks went by and even months had passed and DeShawn continued to pray and the Lord spared her son's life. DeShawn's son went through several months of recovery, surgeries and most of all he suffered a great deal of pain physically as well as mentally, betrayal from one of his best friends, that was deep.

Months had gone by and through a great deal of pain, prayer and suffering God healed all the wounds. Things had just began to return back to normal when all of a sudden DeShawn would receive some very devastating news, news that would change the lives of everyone she loved and those who loved her!

It was two years after DeShawn's son was shot almost to death and his continued recovery. DeShawn returned home from the doctor with the most devastating news. It was four days before DeShawn's 52nd birthday, all was well, DeShawn was planning to celebrate her birthday, remember DeShawn was saved so she wasn't going clubbing however, she did intend to celebrate her life with her friends and family. The news that she received was the worst news that she could have ever received, it was as if she had not been through enough and to hear the doctor say, "DeShawn come into my office and have a seat."

She had been seeing this doctor for over ten years and she had never, ever seen the inside of his office. Whenever DeShawn visited her doctor she always waited in the waiting area to be called by the nurse and then escorted into the examination room, this day the doctor invited DeShawn and her fiance G-man into his official conference office. DeShawn being as observant as she was immediately after being seated said to the doctor, "I have been your patient for over ten years and I have never seen the inside of your office! what's up doc?"

The doctor's reply to DeShawn was, "You're very observant, so I guess this was a dead give away." The doctor continued with, "Yes, DeShawn after completing all of the test and receiving the results of the biopsy I am sorry to inform you that the diagnosis is," and the doctor used some type of doctor's terminology almost like their unreadable hand-writing and DeShawn interrupted with, "Doc, speak english, what are you saying?" and he replied, "DeShawn you have breast cancer!"

Once again DeShawn had to deal with some devastating news. DeShawn looked at her fiance G-man and then at the doctor and stated, "Now what?" The doctor explained DeShawn's options to her and DeShawn explained to the doctor that her birthday was in four days and that she was going home and she would make another appointment to return back to him at that time. DeShawn knew that she had quite a bit of thinking to do along with decisions to be made and prayers that needed to take place.

She knew for sure to take all things to God, whatever decisions that had to take place she would not make any decisions without seeking God's face. DeShawn was a very strong woman and she was well aware of all of her options, but having the moral support of G-man who was now her finace made decision making alittle easier.

DeShawn was well aware of her God, but it was just nice to have someone, a human being to lean on. Yes, G-man was there throughout the entire situation or should I say ordeal. DeShawn celebrated her birthday however, she knew that there was some things and situations that she would have to address, sooner than later.

DeShawn's birthday celebration was over and she called the doctor two days later and made an appointment to see him and G-man was right there by her side. She and G-man prayed together as well as cried together. DeShawn and G-man 'made the decision together to go radical, what's radical? take off the breast! Yeah, that's right, oh vanity, vanity DeShawn.decided to remove the breast. DeShawn kept all of her doctor's, appointments, followed all direction and instructions.

FLY-DI 25
(AFTER IT RAINS, IT POURS)

DeShawn wondered to herself, what the hell could happen next? yeah, she could die, but she knew that God was not through with her yet! She was scheduled to check into the hospital the following Monday^ her family and friends were very uptight but tried to hold their heads.

She was alittle worried not about herself but about her family, her sister was a cry baby and not very strong and her daughters were pitiful, they were scared out of their wits. Her son was still recovering from his gunshot wounds and her nephew, forget it he tried to be strong, but DeShawn knew him and he was afraid too. G-man was as strong as he could be.

The day of the surgery was a day of reckoning, DeShawn was getting ready to have her surgery and everyone was in the waiting area right outside of the operating room, her fiance, sister, children and the pastor and his wife. Everyone was in their own little world! G-man was praying hard, DeShawn never stopped praying and continued to trust her God all the way to the door of the operating room. Her pastor prayed and DeShawn questioned why God had not given her clarity as to what procedure she could use.

The doctor was under the assumption that she was going to have a mastectomy however, God being God all by Hisself waited until the eleventh hour and DeShawn identified with Daniel in the lion's den and Shadrach, Meshach and Abednego in the fiery furnace waiting for God to deliver them. DeShawn waited on a word from God before she went through the doors to the operating room and suddenly the Lord spoke to G-man and He gave him a word, Save The Last For Last, G-man ran to the door and gave her the word that God spoke to him!

DeShawn knowing and understanding the relationship that G-man shared with the Lord DeShawn received the word that was given to G-man for her. She thanked God and informed the doctor that she would not be going radical and that she would be having the second choice which was the lumpdectomy with the removal of two inches of margins all around the area.

The doctor looked at G-man like he had two heads and he looked at DeShawn like she was loosing her mind. The doctor questioned her as to whether she was absolutely sure of the decision that she had made? She replied, "Absolutely I trust God!" The doctor said, "Ok, let's go." He proceed to wheel her through the doors to the operating room. DeShawn remebered her. fiance's last words to her before the doors closed and those words were, "You're going to be just fine because God has you covered and I will be right here when you wake up!"

Through the doors DeShawn went assured that God had her covered and that G-man her fiance would be there when she woke up. The surgery took approximately three hours, the name of the Father, the Son and the Holy Ghost, but to the family and friends that were in the waiting area it probably felt like an eternity. DeShawn could imagine the thoughts that had entered her daughters minds. DeShawn's daughters were not as strong as their mother, she knew that every thing would be alright and whatever she had to go through she would come out a trooper as long as she kept God in the forefront of everything.

DeShawn finally reached the recovery room, all had went well. She continued to be knocked out in another world as a result of anesthesia. The doctor went to the waiting area to inform DeShawn's people that the surgery had gone well. She could just well imagine her family's reaction to the good news. The hardest part was waiting for her to wake up! Again the waiting probably felt like an eternity.

DeShawn finally woke up and everyone that was there when she went under was there when she awoke. The adjustment to the eyes was a little difficult however, a couple of blinks cured that up. DeShawn wasn't surprised to see the people that loved her was truely there when she awoke from the hardest thing she ever had to do in her life.

DeShawn realized that the surgery was only the quiet before the storm. Everyone kept asking her, "How do you feel? Do you feel alright? Do you have any pain?" DeShawn's reply astounded her family when she answered them by saying, "I sure wish they would not have given me those drugs for the pain!" No one could understand where she was coming from with that reply and especially her pastor, but she knew where she was coming from because she had been drug free for a while!

DeShawn was tweeded, I mean feeling no pain and she did not like how the drugs made her feel. She took a stroll down memory lane and it was definitely not a good feeling. The surgery was over and the healing was just the beginning. There was several days of agony, pain, uncertainty, recovery and then the treatment of after the surgery.

DeShawn was -released from the hospital and was scheduled to see the oncologist the doctor who would determine how much radiation and chemotherapy would be needed to complete the entire treatment of breast cancer. When it rains, it pours!

FLY-DI 26
(LET THE CHEMOTHERAPY BEGIN)

DeShawn went through several weeks of radiation and then another twenty weeks of chemo. During the time that DeShawn was going through her radiation treatment she continued to stay strong and trusted God although the radiation wasn't that bad it was the laying on the hard cold table while the radiation technician marked up the area in which he was targeting, the breast that is!

Moving right along, it was the end of the radiation and the beginning of the poison, chemotherapy, the poison that they shoot through your body via veins to destroy any left over cancer cells that may still be lurking to maybe return at a later date in the opposite breast, the same breast or another part of your precious body. Nevertheless, the treatment was necessary for survival. The treatment was very grueling, sometimes you could not eat because eveything you attempted to eat tasted like copper, you know like metallic! Now let's talk about your sense of smell, well everything stunk, yeah that's right stunk. Sometimes DeShawn wondered how much damage was this chemotherapy doing to the rest of her body. The chemotherapy could not differentiate which cells were good and which cells were bad. So once again she to totally rely on the poison finding the appropriate cells to kill and to leave the good guys alone.

DeShawn remembered receiving counseling before she started the treatment, Whoopty-De Doo! No one can prepare anyone for the changes that takes place in a person's body when they go through that crazy, bugged out treatment. Yeah changing lanes caused the rain to pour.

DeShawn was into about the fourth week of her treatment and one of the things she remembered the counselor telling her was that the chemotherapy takes your hair out. Well, it had been four weeks and she still had her hair. Now you must remember how vain DeShawn is, she could not imagine not having any hair however, when she was younger she wore her hair in a low ceasar, you know short cut, little afro as you might call it, but it was by choice. DeShawn could either wait to her hair started falling out or she could make the decision to cut her hair off before the psychologial devastation took place!

The next morning when she attempted to comb her hair and a patch came out in. her hand, it was at that time that the decision had to be madel DeShawn went to the barber shop and demanded that the barber cut all of her hair off down to a low ceasar with a square back, with points on the sides and that's the way it was and it iooked good tool

The barber had a problem with DeShawn cutting off all of her hair, so much so that she decided to tell him the reason for the hair cut. When she shared her ordeal with the barber his reply was, "Wow, you are a strong sister!" DeShawn thanked him, gave him a tip and she exited the shop. Throughout the entire ordeal G-man stuck by her. He went through the good, the bad and the ugly, yes he was right there. G-man stepped up to the plate and handled his business, alcohol, beer and all he was right there. He went to work, payed the mortgage and remember he did not live with her, he resided in the one bedroom apartment down stairs.

It was almost over, the treatment that is. DeShawn and G-man had been discussing marriage and during her illness and recovery G-man was right there so DeShawn decided to except G-man's proposal and they were married on the last day of her treatment. Yes, the last day of her treatment. When DeShawn informed her doctor the oncologist and the nurse that she was getting married on that afternoon they were astonished!

That day was a very special day for DeShawn, not only was it her last day of chemotherapy,, but it was a new beginning for her and G-man and the rest of their lives. Everything that DeShawn had gone through she counted it all joy, why? because she was still alive, she was getting married and she. thanked God for wigs. Everything was in place and DeShawn's wedding was fabulous, you never would have believed that the day of DeShawn's wedding was the last day of her chemo, she was a beautiful bride.

DeShawn and her bridal party dressed at her sister's house in Brooklyn, there were limos, photographers and the whole nine yards. DeShawn was very excited and most of all she-was not sick or tired from her last chemo treatment. Once again God had given DeShawn favor.

The wedding was being held at the church that DeShawn and G-man both attended, the church where she was a minister and G-man was a fine deacon, oh praise his name. DeShawn did the norm and was about an hour late for her wedding, but she looked beautiful.

When she arrived at the church some of her guest had become impatient and was standing outside, but when DeShawn stepped out of the limousine she could hear the oohs and ahhs as the people exclaimed how beautiful DeShawn looked. DeShawn felt so good and most of all it was a day that she would never forget.

As she entered into the church the congregation was instructed to stand to their feet when the bride entered. DeShawn remembered the look on G-man's face when he turned around to watch his bride enter, the look that was on G-man's face DeShawn would never forget; G-man looked as though he was a kid in a candy store. The smile that was on G-man's face was something to reckon with, he was indeed very happy. The bible states, "When a man finds a wife he finds a good thing."

FLY-DI 27
(DeShawn's Wedding Vows)

Well DeShawn was his good thing! In spite of everything that DeShawn had gone through and having her last treatment the day of her wedding it was very hard to tell that she had been through all of what she had gone through.

The church that DeShawn and G-man confessed their vows in was a very small church and almost all the members were related to one another, but here we were standing in the middle of this little church on "this glorious day when DeShawn noticed that the pastor who stood in front of her, G-man and the entire congregation had a slightly aggravated look on his face because she had arrived at the church almost two hours late, oh well!

The wedding commenced and G-man and DeShawn confessed their love and promised to love, cherish, honor and obey until death do them part and they both agreed and then the pastor said, "I now pronounce you husband and wife." DeShawn remembered thinking to herself; now why did I agree to honor and obey? she felt like there should have been a stipulation in there like, obey and agree only if what you're honoring and obeying really makes' sense. DeShawn knew that there were times when her and G-man disagreed on a lot of things and to talk about obeying, well that was a horse of another color.

The pastor then said, "You may kiss your bride." DeShawn remembered G-man kissing her like there was no tomorrow. The pastor then said, "I now introduce Mr. and Mrs. G-man to the church and congregation." Everyone then stood up and suddenly all DeShawn remembered seeing were flashes from all the cameras as the congregation began taking pictures. I know I look good wig and all, but enough already she thought to herself as she continued to smile and pose for the picture takers.

After the wedding the reception followed immediately at DeShawn's house. Everything was beautiful especially the decorations, everything was going according to plan except for one thing, DeShawn had allowed a friend of hers' who professed to be a caterer prepare the food, well let me tell you the food arrived three hours late! By the time the food arrived it was like a take out. The guest were leaving and taking their food out with -them. DeShawn was very annoyed, once again it seemed as if every time she attempted to help someone she always managed toget jerked in the process, story of DeShawn's life, help other people, get jerked!

All in all the reception turned out well, DeShawn and G-man received alot of monetary gifts seeing as how DeShawn was already keeping house and G-man was renting the one bedroom apartment in the basement. DeShawn was very happy and she made such a beautiful bride in spite of! Almost everything went according to plan, everyone was very happy.

DeShawn was very happy and so was G-man. Everyone ha.d left and the reception was over. G-man and DeShawn was all alone. DeShawn remembered G-man expressing his feelings as he cried in DeShawn's arms. He began to tell her how proud he was of her and how beautiful she looked as his wife and bride. He also questioned where she had received such strength. DeShawn remembered telling G-man that her strength comes from above. G-man slept upstairs that night and DeShawn said to G-man, "I now pronouce you husband and wife, you may kiss your bride!" Those were the sweetest words that had ever been said.

FLY-DI 28
(NEW BEGINNINGS)

This was the beginning of their lives together! G-man moved upstairs and they began to share their lives together. DeShawn began to learn how to share her space and that was very difficult for her. DeShawn had been alone for a long time and taking orders or should I say taking directions was very hard for DeShawn. She had been her own boss for a long time and the adjustment was very difficult. DeShawn also realized that the sharing of space was very hard for G-man too because he had lived alone for a long time as well. Both G-man and DeShawn realized that there was going to be a great deal of adjustment that would have to be made however, they were both willing to give it a shot. They realized to make every effort to allow for all mistakes and to take all mistakes in love for the most part and it was working out pretty well.

G-man was a very intelligent man, he could hold a conversation in any area whether it was black history, religion, economics, war or poverty. G-man was wise beyond his years and that was one of the attributes that attracted DeShawn to G-man, he was the first man that she had met in a long time that was able to stimulate her with intelligent conversation. Yeah, G-man was exciting and he was able to hold DeShawn's interest and to her that was a miracle. Most brothers DeShawn had come in contact with either talked out the side of their mouth, you know that slick Rick stuff or they were talking about how good she look and what they would like to do to her.

G-man and DeShawn developed their relationship through stimulating conversation and friendship. They had a lot in common they knew how to share intimacy and not intercourse. You see there's so many people that confuse intercourse with intimacy and we should be aware of the fact that there is a difference.

The intimacy that G-man and DeShawn shared equaled closeness in minds and thoughts, closeness and familiarity, and intercourse for them was communication, exchange of thoughts, services, feelings and then a sexual connection. DeShawn trusted G-man explicityly and G-man trusted her.

As time marched on all in all things seemed to be going along fine, at least that is what DeShawn was thinking not realizing that G-man was having issues with the fact that he moved into DeShawn's house and that it was not a house that they had purchased together. You see G-man was a real man, you know every man that puts on a pair of pants does not constitute a man! G-man had his own dreams, wants and desires. G-man wanted to purchase a house for us,

81

in both our names and he had a burning desire to relocate to Florida. DeShawn thought that G-man's dream was her dream as well, but it really wasn't.

DeShawn had a dream of her own, she wanted to start a program/Boarding Home for Men who had been incarcerated for fifteen years or more. Her program was going to be the home that these men could look forward to upon their release. G-man at first had been in agreement with DeShawn and her dream and then suddenly all of the negativity began to surface. G-man started saying things like, "We're too old to start another career, we're relocating to Florida." Well needless to say that the only thing that was important to G-man was relocating to Florida, her dreams were no longer important to G-man or should I say it became a back burner issue with G-man.

He attempted to show some interest in the program however, it was not real, he tried very hard to act interested even down to attempting to encourage DeShawn to follow her dreams. G-man did the best he could. In reality G-man and DeShawn's plans were totally different. Time was moving on and for the first couple of years everything seemed to be working out as well as could be expected, the thing that made the adjustments easier was the mere fact that DeShawn and G-man respected what each one stood for.

DeShawn encouraged G-man to follow his dreams and he encouraged her to do the same. If you remember back in the earlier chapters DeShawn talked about when it rains, it pours? well it started pouring in DeShawn's life once again. Say what, yeah that's what I said, if it was not enough that DeShawn had gotten sick and had to have treatment and a healing process, but here we go again!

G-man and DeShawn were watching T.V. one night and G-man began to moan, G-man had a high tolerance for pain and that was a dead give away for G-man, that is how DeShawn knew that G-man was in a great deal of pain. G-man began holding his chest, DeShawn began to question where the pain was. G-man stated that the pain was in his chest and that his arm was feeling numb, DeShawn quickly realized that her husband was suffering a heart attack, when it rains it pours!

DeShawn immediately attempted to comfort her husband and at the same time informing him that she was going to call 911, G-man resisted but DeShawn paid him no mind, she called 911. When the ambulance arrived that confirmed her biggest fear that her husband was in fact having a heart attack. The ambulance attendant took his pulse, checked his blood pressure and immediately gave him a EKG, the results of the EKG made the ambulance attendant act hastefully. He informed G-man that he had to go to the hospital immediately. G-man did not want to go to the hospital, the attendant began to explain to G-man how serious his situation was. DeShawn remembered the attendant saying to G-man, "Sir, we can not waste any time, this is serious."

Yeah, when it rains it pours! G-man had a heart attack. They rushed him to the emergency room and began running tests on him. DeShawn began asking questions like, "How serious is this? what is the next procedure? where is the heart specialist?" DeShawn was right by G-man's side just as he was for her.

That night DeShawn remained at the hospital all night, DeShawn refused to leave her husband's side. DeShawn questioned every move the doctor or the nurses made. DeShawn would not allow them to do anything to G-man without running it by her first. She asked for clarity when there was something that she did not understand.

G-man tried to be brave and he acted as though he was handling the whole situation, there was no fear exhibited on G-man's face however, DeShawn could read his heart, he was afraid, G-man had a way with hisself, he was good at disguising his true feelings.

Well, the dodo hit the fan! G-man was informed that he-needed to have a procedure done which would allow them to view the heart valves, well low and behold they attempted to perform the procedure and they punctured the vein and they had to discontinue the procedure.

During the entire ordeal DeShawn was praying to God arid requested God's presence in that emergency room on that night. DeShawn was well aware of the fact that she could ask anything in God's name and that it would be given unto her. DeShawn asked God to save her husband and to guide the doctor's hands in anything they did where it regarded all procedures performed on her husband. DeShawn's faith is so strong in God that she knew that anything that she asked in Jesus name it would come to pass. God is.a good God, oh yes he is.

G-man knew God for hisself and he was also aware of the fact that he was married to a prayed up woman. DeShawn's healing was in her praise. In spite of what she was going through DeShawn relied on God for everything. She knew that God's word would never come back void. God is a God of love and understanding and God knew that DeShawn loved G-man with the type of love that God taught us. For God so loved the world, that he gave his only begotten Son, that whosoever believed in him should not perish, but have everlasting life. St.John 3:16.

G-man was very much familiar with God and his perfect love. That night was a very long night, G-man finally fell asleep and the Lord came to G-man in his sleep and directed him not to allow the doctors to perform any more procedures on him. The doctors wanted to perform a by-pass on G-man's heart and G-man informed DeShawn that he heard God speak to him and God told G-man not to have the procedure. The doctors attempted to talk DeShawn into talking G-man into having the procedure however, she respected G-man's relationship with God and she respected his decision to pass on the by-pass.

During the emergency room stay G-man's doctor in the emergency room was a 'young Jewish doctor who was very good in his field, look at God! He attended to G-man and treated him during his stay in-the emergency room and he gave us his office telephone number and directed DeShawn to.bring G-man to his office when he was discharged. G-man was discharged the following day and DeShawn made an appointment to see the young Jewish doctor at his office.

Watch God work, when we arrived at the doctor's office he shared an office with a cardiologist, a heart doctor, look at God! "Now unto him that is able to do exceeding abundantly above all that we ask or think, according to the power that worketh in us." **Ephesians 3:20.** A cardiologist right in the same office, and it gets better! G-man was seen by the cardiologist on the same day. G-man was given another EKG and it was determined that G-man did not even need a by-pass. DeShawn prayed day and night for G-man her husband because she knew that we should "pray one for another, that ye may be healed. The effectual fervent prayer of a righteous man or woman availeth much." **James 5:16.**

G-man recovered and after awhile things went back to normal. G-man felt that God had granted him a new lease on life and he was going to live his life to the fullest. He began to hang out more, drink and continued to smoke his kools, yeah he thought hanging out was cool and that he deserved to live life to the fullest.

DeShawn had a whole different concept to living life to the fullest. Living life to the fullest for DeShawn was each and every day that she awoke to a brand new day and nobody had to roll her over, change her pamper, on feed her and she could place her feet on the ground and put one foot after the other, now that was living life to the fullest.

G-man was living like some one owed him something and he had set out to get it. The relationship began to deteriorate. DeShawn would worry herself sick each and everytime G-man would go hanging out, she knew that everytime G-man hung out he would drink and might I add he would return home drunk as a skunk! DeShawn's biggest concern was G-man driving while intoxicated and killing himself or some innocent person. Everytime G-man went out DeShawn could not sleep until he was back safely in the house, this went on month after month.

DeShawn and G-man verbally fought all the time. DeShawn, remembered one day G-man came home and he was high again, mind you he had stopped going to church, there was no more prayer and worship or should I say if he was doing prayer and worship it was no longer visible or audible to DeShawn.

Yeah, G-man thought he had it all together and when he. was drinking out of the abundance of the heart his mouth spoke. DeShawn began to question whether G-man had a death wish or. something, she began to tell him how God had blessed him and how he should be grateful to be alive. G-man looked at DeShawn and acclaimed, "You know DeShawn you are relentless, you never stop running your mouth, the only thing you talk about is <u>Jesus, Jesus, Jesus!</u> **That's the only thing that comes out of your mouth!** Life is filled with other things besides Jesus, Jesus, Jesus! He even quoted scripture to DeShawn reminding her of God wanting us to have life and have it more abundantly, oh he was well versed in the scriptures.

DeShawn could not believe that G-man had spoken such garbage out of his mouth! She was shocked, appallled and needless to say she was livid, those was fighting words to DeShawn.

DeShawn was so glad that she knew how to pray and to be able to get a prayer through at the drop of a dime.

She began to pray for G-man on the spot, she interceded for him requesting God's forgiveness for the things that G-man spoke out his mouth where it regarded Jesus, Jesus, Jesus. There was a change that had taken place in G-man, he was not the same man that DeShawn had met and married. He did a total 360 degrees' turn in the opposite direction and that was sad, after all the Lord had done for him, he saved him and kept him alive and he didn't even have to have surgery! Well, I think that is enough to shout up and down about, don't you? But apparently it didn't phase G-man, what would it take to snap him back to reality? DeShawn realized that God has a calling on G-man's life however, G-man has to realize it.

As time went on GTman remained the same arid their marriage desolved at G-man's request. G-man decided that part of him wanted to stay with DeShawn and part of him wanted to leave. After much prayer and a great deal of fasting on DeShawn's part G-man took the part of him that wanted to stay and caught it up with the part of him that wanted to leave and no matter how much fasting and praying DeShawn did G-man left.

DeShawn remembered how she felt when G-man gave her the crap about part of him' wanted to stay and part of him wanted to leave, she recalled telling G-man if he .wanted to play catch up then catch up the part of him that wanted to stay and catch it up with the part that wanted to leave and boogie. DeShawn never really thought that G-man really wanted to leave, but G-man left and moved back to Kings County Brooklyn and he wasted no time, it was almost as if he previously planned to move.

DeShawn remembered being so angry however, she remembered what **Ephesians 4:26** dictated, "Be ye angry, and sin not, let not the sun go down upon your wrath." DeShawn was very upset, she was so upset she kept wondering when she was going to break down and cry, she was waiting for the sleepless nights and the inability to eat, 'never happened.' she could not understand why she was not suffering from any of the above symptons.

Days, weeks, months and now a whole year had passed and DeShawn continued to wait for some type of emotion and then one day DeShawn began thinking about timing and how everything has its' own time. **Ecclesiastes 3:1** states, "To everything there is a season, and a time to every purpose under the heaven." Well, DeShawn realized that G-man was placed in her life just for a season. She never heard the Holy Ghost speak to her informing her that G-man was her husband nor did G-man hear from God informing him that DeShawn was his wife.

DeShawn continued to pray and seek God's face as to why she was not suffering from her separation until one day while she was praying she received a word from the Lord which said, "The reason that there are no tears and no pain is because you chose him, I did not send him to you for marriage I sent him for your season and his season as well." DeShawn realized that their season was just to take care of one another in their time of need.

Time moved on and once again she was all alone and it felt right. DeShawn continued to go to work, go to church, attend', bible study and back home she went. She continued to keep God first in her life, yes it was all about Jesus, Jesus, Jesus!' Things were going pretty good at work and DeShawn's finances were ok so she decided to treat herself to a new car. DeShawn had been driving an old Malibu so she up graded her car to a 2004 Nissan Sentra however, after driving the Sentra and realizing that the back seats were too small for tall people she decided to trade in her 2004 Sentra for a 2005 Altama and in doing so DeShawn met a man who was employed at the dealership and they began to see each other and it really felt nice.

He believed in God, he attended church with DeShawn and was even baptised and he joined the church! DeShawn was very happy and things were going good. When DeShawn purchased her car Charlie allowed her to use his discount which dropped the price of the car tremendously. Charlie was a very sweet man.

DeShawn explained to Charlie that she was a preacher and the fact that she was sold out to God and could not have sex with him. Charlie appeared to be alright with the fact that they could not be intimate sexually.

They continued to date and attend church every Sunday together. Things appeared to be going fine. History was repeating itself, it was like deja vu, Charlie moved in and began renting the one bedroom apartment in the basement, yes the same one bedroom apartment G-man used to, rent before they were married. Charlie was a very humble and caring man, a very giving man. All was good, a year went by and Charlie and DeShawn became engaged, history repeating itself. It appeared to DeShawn that whenever things were going good.for her something happens! What hapened now, when it rains it pours that had become her motto, When it rains it pours.

FLY-DI 29
(LEARNING TO LIVE WITHOUT HER FATHER)

DeShawn's father took ill and it was very strange because to just look at him he did not look ill and he did not act ill however, he was very ill. DeShawn had to run back and forth to the doctor with her father and guess who did all the running with DeShawn? it was Charlie! She took her father from doctor to doctor and they kept telling DeShawn that her father might be suffering from dementia, she told the doctors that she was not interested in what they thought, she wanted to know what they knew for sure. She directed the doctors to schedule her father for an M.R.I, and Cat Scan of the brain, well you know DeShawn never went to medical school, Oh bless the Lord for God will give you wisdom and that is what DeShawn needed to go to the next level with her father and his health.

It took approximately sixty nine days for DeShawn's father to go through all that he went through. DeShawn was informed that her father had a malignant brain tumor. The doctor went on to say that he could do surgery on his brain and that the tumor was so large that he may not be able to get it all. When DeShawn informed her father of the doctor's findings he made her promise that she would not allow the doctors to operate on his head. DeShawn's questioned her father's decision but he was adamant about his decision and he went on to explain how he intended to go back to the father with every part that he came here with! DeShawn was very happy with her father's decision. She did not want the doctors sawing through her father's head to get to his skull to reach his brain. At 83 years old he never would have made it, but the doctor would have been able to purchase a new boat or another summer home with the cost of that type of surgery, bam! wrong person, not her daddy! So the decision was made and that was it, that's all folks!

Two days later DeShawn's father was transferred from a Queens hospital where they could not do anything else for him because they stated that the hospital was for sick people and DeShawn's father was not sick he was terminal, well! so they transferred him to a wonderful hospice house in the only borough with **The** in front of it, The Bronx! where they took very good care of him.

Deja vu all over again. DeShawn was at work on that dreadful day when the hospice called DeShawn and advised her to summon all family members and come to the hospice immediately. DeShawn began to call the family and informed them of the information she had just received. AJiter gathering the family they all arrived at the bedside of her daddy, her sister, her nephew and of course Charlie.

They all gathered around the bedside of DeShawn's father. For someone who was suffering from brain cancer God had it so that he was never in any pain. Yeah, that's right, that's what I said, he was never in any pain. He always looked as though he was at peace with meeting his maker.

As they stood by his bedside he began to talk to them in a very low tone. He instructed DeShawn that when he met his demise he wanted his pastor to officiate the service however, he said if his pastor was unable to officiate the service he did not want anyone else but DeShawn to do it. DeShawn felt honored that her father felt enough of her to want her to officiate his home going service. DeShawn remembered praying that whenever God saw fit to take her father home that the big renown preacher who her father diligently payed tithes to on a monthly basis would be there to deliver the eulogy.

Well, as they sat and prayed with pop he appeared to be comfortable, after praying with her dad DeShawn went down stairs to the store, yes her and Charlie left for five minutes and suddenly her cell phone began to ring, it was her nephew directing her to return to the room immediately. DeShawn questioned her nephew, "What's wrong? what's the matter?" her nephew exclaimed, "Come right now!"

By the time DeShawn left the store that was right across the street and arrived back to her father's room he had already passed away. DeShawn was so glad that she was not present when he passed. DeShawn's sister and nephew informed DeShawn that her father had appeared to have lost his vision for a second and then he looked up, smiled and went home to be with the Lord! How do I know that he went home to be with the Lord? what else, would he have been smiling about!

DeShawn was very happy that her father met his demise with a smile on his face. She was so grateful that her and her father had made amends because she truly loved her father however, she was not please with the way he lived his life.

DeShawn remembered feeling real bad about not calling her fathers' companion to accompany them to her father's bedside, it was not done on purpose contrary to popular opinion! She ;-just gravitated to her immediate family. When DeShawn did inform her father's companion of his demise, DeShawn was not too sure whether the companion was shocked, happy or sad, well everyone reacts differently to death!

DeShawn had to make funeral arrangements, her father had already placed his paper work in order long before his illness. DeShawn's dad had already had a mausoleum that he had purchased several years prior to his death and when her mother met her demise all DeShawn had to do was to reopen it. DeShawn's father use to say that he refused to be buried in the ground because he was sick and tired of people throwing dirt in his face. DeShawn thought what a strange statement! It was very surprising to her to hear her father talk about being tired of having dirt thrown in his face especially since as far as she was concerned with all the low down, dirty, grimy, stinking filthy dirt that he continued to throw in her mother's face, hum, what goes around comes around. DeShawn for one second thought about burying her father in the same grave with her mother because she knew that would have made her mother happy because she lived and died with her husband in her heart in spite of who he was and the things he did.

DeShawn once again applied scripture to her life and her decision and she over came evil with good, **Romans 12:21.** DeShawn continued to make the funeral arrangements for her father.

She called the big renown preacher from her father's prestigious church. DeShawn remembered speaking to a secretary, who transferred her to the busines manager who took the urgent message of her father's death for her pastor. DeShawn waited for a return call from the pastor that never came.

She remembered sharing her feelings with her sister about having to preside over their father's going home service. Her sister recalled a time while they were visiting with dad that he had actually given DeShawn the topic which he wanted her to preach from, strangely enough he wanted DeShawn to preach on family, wow, that was deep.

DeShawn trusted her sister's interpretation of what she heard their dad's request was. What is family? DeShawn began to ponder, family constituted a father, a mother and their children, children of the same house, a group of people living in the same house! No matter how she looked at that picture it was going to be very hard she thought for her to preach around family when the love of her life was still incarcerated, you remember DeShawn's brother, and now her dad who deep down in her heart she really loved had met. his demise! How was she going to do it she thought to herself. In her family the father was never around, some how he was always M.I.A., you know missing in action. His action wasn't with the family it was always somewhere else, with someone else.

DeShawn was determine to do what needed to be done and her sister was counting on her. Once again she relied on her God and his word toget her through. She remembered what **Proverbs 3:5-6** stated, "Trust in the Lord with all thine heart, and lean not unto thine own understanding, in all thy ways acknowledge Him and He shall direct they paths", and believe me DeShawn was counting on Him.

The day of the funeral had finally come, DeShawn was prayed up and she knew that God would be right where she needed Him to be. DeShawn was attending a new church for over a year and the members of her new church were in attendance, there were family members and friends that she did not know, but for some reason they knew who she was and they all arrived at the same conclusion and that was she looked just like her father.

DeShawn's brother was allowed to attend the services however, the pastor from DeShawn's old church that she had attended for seven years, the church that she was married in did not even show! Oh well, that was alright, DeShawn was determine that all she needed was God and she would be alright.

The order of service was as followed, the processional, first family and then friends, congregational hymn, scripture old testament, new testament, prayer of comfort, solo/selection, remarks/acknowledgement of cards and condolences, the obituary, song of inspiration and then the eulogy.

DeShawn began to speak about family! If I must say so myself! DeShawn talked about family uniting and become as one as God intended. She also talked about traders in the camp, the camp called family. That did not go over well, only the traders felt offended, but DeShawn gave them what her father on earth had given her before his demise and her father in heaven.

Her new pastor gave the benediction, prayer of departure and the service was over. All was well except for one thing, DeShawn's father and his sister were not speaking for a long time over a very foolish thing, money! The sad part about it was they never made amends before he met his demise so his sister was left to deal with that. Guess what the bible states that it's the love of money that's the sin, **1st Timothy 6:10,** and you know something I never seen a Brinks truck follow a hearse!

Everything was over and after the funeral everyone went their separate ways. The extended family on DeShawn's fathers' side who had not seen each other in years did not even swap telephone numbers and they were first cousins, well you can tell that they were not listening to the speech on family, moving right along.

DeShawn attempted to get her life back on track however, her father had left so much unfinished business so she really did not have time to grieve her father's death until much later. She did not attend church for about two weeks and guess what? her pastor told her when she returned to church that the Holy Ghost told her to sit DeShawn down; what that means is DeShawn was not allowed to preach. Well, you know that was not of God, that was personal.

God does not work backwards, God was well aware of the fact that DeShawn was grieving her father's death and she could not come out to the church's anniversary; that was not God's stuff, that was the pastot's stuff. DeShawn did not debate the situation, she took all of her clergy robes and left. DeShawn went back to her old church because she knew that day she needed to be surrounded by the sisters and brothers of God, not of the church.

We all know that there are church goers, those are the folks that go to church out of habit, and then there are church members, those who attend and join the church because that's the church that their family use to attend then there's DeShawn who attends church for strength and healing and deliverance.

FLY-DI 30
(CHURCH, WHAT IS IT?)

Church is where a group of Christians worship and hold religious services, a group of Christians with the same beliefs and under the same authority and that authority is not man or woman, it's God! When a person attends a church they should be able to seek the face of the Lord in spite of. The church should be able to reach out to the person and welcome them without opinion. Church folk they have a habit of judging people, they probably for got where they came from. Some church folk are so heavenly bound till they are no earthly good!

DeShawn had been saved and delivered for twenty years and she was a fine preacher, she preached only what she was anointed to preach and no more.

She looked at the church as a place of recovery, a hospital for the sick, a place where you go when there is no place else . to go. The church, what is it really? The bible states in **Acts 2;47** that it's a place of "Praising God, and having favour with all people, and the Lord will add to the church daily such as should be saved", but tell me how can the people praise God and receive favour and add to the church and become saved when the folk in the church worship man instead of Godl Yeah, that's deep, the folk in the church run around prophesying, speaking in unknown tongues and won't even speak to the sister or brother sitting next to them, check that out, Hallelujah! Deep ain't it? Yes, it's real and it's happening.

Being wounded in the house of the Lord is devastating and it really hurts. People in the church can really tear you apart if you are not strong in the Lord and the power of his might. There is also a great deal of jealousy, malice and envy among the preachers, elders, deacons and evangelist and that just won't work.

Mark 9:50 states that we should "have peace one with another." DeShawn has been saved, yes some people may say saved, what is that? Was she lost? Yes, she was, she was lost in the madness of the cardinal world and one day twenty years ago she heard God speak to her; yes to her and He said, "Come out from among them and be ye separated...."**2nd Corinthians 6:17.**

DeShawn answered that.call from God and began serving Him with her whole heart! Let me tell you something, it was not easy to serve God and think that from that point on everything was going to be peachy creme, I got news for you! She caught more hell in the churches than she did in the clubs, yeah, that's right, that's what I said!. Hanging out in the clubs was cool and the gang, there was never any problems until the get high ran out! When the get high' ran out the only problems they had was figuring out where th£ next get high was going to come from.

In churches there is always some drama, whether it's a pastor stuck in his old fashion ways that a woman preacher should be seen but not heard, or you have another preacher that feels threatened because the congregation responded better to the female preacher than they responded to him. Well now ain't that some crap.

Then you got some pastors that attempt to control your mind, Oh I know you guys are aware of the preacher and the 'kool-aid', yeah that story, Jim Jones, you know they all drank the kool-aid that the pastor gave them and they all died. Umm, that's why you have to know God for yourself.

Moving right along, then you got some folk that's been in the church since the year of the flood, what you talking about? Those folk who been in the same church, in the same seat forever! Don't let a new person or visitor come in the church and attempt to sit in sister so and so's seat, "Oh, no baby that's my seat" or "that's sister so and so's seat." Now, you done chased a new person out of the church with your nasty attitude about a seat.

DeShawn had lost so many people in her family who were very dear to her and she had threw herself into the church and her God. She had expected the church family to be a lot different than they were, she never realized that there were so many hell raisers in the church.

Now let's talk a little bit about the 3 P's, **Preaching, Pimping, Pastors,** the pastors that preach and do theatrics, Well what do you mean by that? PPP's are preachers that preach a fine word, they come from the bible and then they let themselves get involved and they begin to say something like this, "God said there's 30 people in here" (it's around offering time) "that has $100 dollars, come now, come right now and get the blessing that God has for you." First of all if there were 30 people with $100 dollars and God said it, there would be no prompting, no tricks, no gimmicks, no games, the 30 people would be popping up like popcorn, Oh bless his name! Oh don't get me wrong there are seed offerings, first fruit offerings and offerings but you got to know the difference.

Alright, I told you about the PPP's now let me tell you about the preachers that tell you that they do not want you speaking in tongues in his church, Yeah you heard what I said, see the bible states in **St. Marks 16:17** "And these signs shall follow them that believe, in My name shall they cast out devils, they shall speak with new tongues", and if you need further proof, **Acts 19:6** states, "When Paul had laid his hands upon them, the Holy Ghost came on them, and they spoke with tongues, and prophesied", so if that is not enough proof then I don't know what to tell you! So if you attend a church that does not allow you to speak in tongues you need to put on a pair of skates and roll up out of there.

Now that we have gotten passed speaking in tongues let's talk a little bit about the preachers that dangle ordination in front of your face like dangling a carrot in front of a rabbit!

They promise to ordain you which will allow you to perform weddings, funerals, christenings and the Lord's Supper; you know the wine and bread that we take on the first Sunday of the month, **1st Corinthians 11:24-25,** "And when He had given thanks, He broke it and said, "Take, eat; this is My body which is broken for you; do this in remembrance of Me." "In the same manner also He took the cup, when He had supped, saying, "This cup is the new testament in MY blood, this do ye, as often as ye drink it in remembrance of Me." Yeah, if the preacher knows your desire they will hold.it over your head.

Also be careful of the preacher or pastor that tells you that God told them to ordain you, Oh yeah DeShawn went through that too and then they come back with a story why they are not going to ordain you at the said time!

Then you have the pastor that brings you in front of the board members and charges you with some bogus charges like you was disrespectful to your leader, or you spoke out of line. So you go in front of the board and the board finds no fault in you an the pastor really gets upset, oh well!

All DeShawn wanted to do was worship and praise the Lord for all of his wonderful works and favour. When you are under a pastor that feels threatened by you he can make your life a living hell! Yeah, that's what I said, you heard me. Whether your pastor is male or female it can be a night mare.

Then you have the First Lady, who is the First Lady? That's the pastor's wife, now that's a horse of a different color. I attempted to study where the title First Lady came from biblically and I could find nothing! Well I don't know everything but one thing I know for sure is that the First Lady can really get carried away in that title, don't get me wrong, not all First Ladies are the same. Some are sweet, understanding and there for you, and then you have others who think they are tuff, they will even stand over you, get in your face and pop ghetto garbage and nothing happens to them, they are not brought up in front of the board or anything, and what's worst is when they are not even sat down, which means that they are not able to function in their title for a specific time.

The good thing about it all is that God sits high ami He sees low so He is aware of all things that take place. That is why DeShawn continued to remain focus and contirmed to stay in her bible and remembered the word of God in **Psalms 121:1-2?** "I will lift up mine eyes unto the hills from whence cometh my help", "My help cometh from the Lord, which made heaven and earth." Yes, you got to know God for yourself!

Now I want to warn you about the Deacons. The deacons are the pastor's, the male-pastors right hand men! They walk, talk and think like their pastor. Yes, the church is suppose to capture the pastor's vision however, they should be able to think for theirselves.

Last but not least be careful with the men in the congregation that make this statement, **"God told me",** Oh be careful with that. What you will hear the most is "God told me that you are my wife." Yeah, funny ha-ha, everyone that cries holy is not holy and God warns us about false prophets, **St. Matthew 24:11**, "And many false prophets shall rise, and shall deceive many." So I say again, Church, what is it? It is what you make it, that's it and that's all.

DeShawn went through a great deal of trials and tribulations in the house of the Lord. She knew that all she wanted to do was to thank God for all that he had done for her. He was a mother to the motherless, a father to the fatherless, He was a way out of no-way, He was the lifter of her head, He was her hope for tomorrow and the wheel in the middle of the wheel, He was her water when she was thirsty, and He was her shepherd and she would not want, He made her to lie down in green pastures, He lead her beside still waters, He restored her soul, He leadeth her in the paths of righteousness for His name sake, DeShawn knew that yea, though she walked through the valley of the shadow of death, she feared no evil for she knew thou art with her, thy rod and thy staff they comforted her, He preparest a table before her in the presence of her enemies, thou anointed her head with oil, her cup runneth over, and surely goodness and mercy will follow her all the days of her life and she will dwell in the house of the Lord forever! Yeah, that is a hell of a promise from God and it was enough for DeShawn.

One thing we must remember is that every church is not the same and every pastor is not the same. You have to become aware of the reason why you are going to church and who you are worshipping when you attend church, is it man or woman or God? Need I tell you what a wonderful, smart Bishop instructed DeShawn to do: "1. Keep your eyes on the prize and the prize is Jesus, 2. Don't put your pastor higher than he aught to be!" DeShawn learned a very valuable lesson and if she didn't remember anything else she remembered numbers 1 & 2, keep your eyes on the prize and not to place her pastor higher than he aught to be.

She also remembered that holiness is not something that we put on, it's something that we are willing to livel It's not so important to carry **God's name as it is to carry God's Nature!**

DeShawn is still attending church and it's twenty years later and she continues to follow the rule, Keep your eyes on the prize and put no man or. woman higher than they aught to be and always remember that- church is in your heart, not in a building!

Last but definitely not least, **Hebrews 10:25,** "Not forsaking the assembling of ourselves together, as the manner of some is, but exhorting one another, and so much more, as ye see the day approaching." **Psalms 133:1**, "Behold how good and how pleasant it is for brethren to dwell together in unity." **Hebrews 3:4**, "For every house is built by some man, but He that built all things is God." "For God is not the author of confusion but of peace, as in all the churches of the saints." **1st Cornithians 14:33,** So it's very important to study, "To show thyself approved unto God, a workman needeth not be ashame, rightly dividing the word of truth." **2nd Timothy 2:15.**

So the saga continues in the churches, but DeShawn will continue to bless the Lord at all times and his praises shall continuously be in her mouth and this song will continue to play in her heart, **The Spirit Of The Lord Is; Here, I, Can Feel Him In The Atmosphere**!